About the author

PEONY BROWN

Delve into the world of Peony Brown, an enchanting storyteller whose vibrant life has been brimming with meaningful connections and cherished experiences. Hailing from a remarkable collective of gifted songwriters, Peony is devoted to capturing the art of storytelling in a series of heartwarming narratives focused on family. Her narratives are a testament to the profound impact of love, illuminating its ability to shape and fortify individuals and their familial bonds. Accompany Peony Brown on these captivating odysseys as she unveils a tapestry of love, family, and invaluable life teachings. As Peony Brown and her team continue to share these seeds of love, they have encountered and been able to witness with everyone.

The Last Note

PEONY BROWN

EXIT 26 PUBLISHING

Contents

Chapter 1

Dean Winchester's heart raced as he navigated the chaotic kitchen, balancing a towering tray of greasy dishes with expert precision. The heat and noise were suffocating, and the constant shouts and clatter of pots and pans added to the chaos. Sweat dripped down his forehead as he tried to keep up with the frantic pace, and the sharp smells of cooking food and burning oil made him dizzy.

"Order up!" someone shouted, but Dean barely registered it over the pounding in his ears. He couldn't help but feel a thrill of adrenaline rush through him, reminiscent of the high he got when performing on stage. But those dreams were distant now, buried under the weight of his responsibilities and obligations to his job as a busboy.

As he reached for his pocket, hoping for a momentary respite from the commotion, the head chef's booming voice shattered his thoughts.

"Dean, table five needs clearing!" he barked, causing Dean to flinch in surprise.

"Got it," Dean called back, his grip tightening on the stack of dishes as he weaved through the crowded kitchen toward table five. His mind was still curious about the constant buzzing from his phone, but now all thoughts were consumed by one singular goal – getting through this shift.

With each cleared table and pile of dirty dishes, Dean could feel the weight of his yet unfulfilled dreams bearing down on him. But he determinedly pushed them aside, focusing on providing for himself and those he cared about.

"I just cleared that table five," Dean announced upon returning to the kitchen, aware that one missed call from his roommates could mean a new opportunity or another crushing disappointment. But no matter what lay ahead, he knew those friends would support and push him forward, just as they always had.

The sharp clatter of silverware hitting the tiled floor jolted Dean from his thoughts. He quickly sprang into action, scooping up the fallen utensils with a sense of urgency that matched the frantic beat of his heart. It had been pounding relentlessly in his chest since he received the text message, its urgent tone echoing in his mind.

As he returned the fork and knife to their rightful place, Dean couldn't help but glance around the bustling restaurant, searching for any signs of respite from his duties. But there was none to be found, and Dean knew he couldn't afford to let his guard down.

"Hey, Dean," whispered Jenny, one of his co-workers, sidling beside him with a knowing grin. You seem pretty distracted today. Is everything okay?"

Dean forced a smile that didn't quite reach his eyes. "Uh, yeah," he replied. "Just got a text from my roommates. They need me to call them right away." He hesitated before adding anxiously, "I'm thinking about that."

Jenny's eyebrows furrowed in concern. "Can you take a quick break? I'll cover for you."

But Dean shook his head, feeling the weight of responsibility pressing down on him like a thick fog. "I can't risk it. The manager's been watching me like a hawk. I'll have to wait until my break."

"Okay," Jenny said, reassuringly squeezing his arm understandingly before disappearing into the busy dining room.

"Thanks, Jenny," Dean murmured gratefully as he returned to the clearing tables.

With a deep breath, he pushed aside his worries and forced himself back into work mode, deftly stacking plates and glasses with practiced precision. But as each minute passed without any news from his roommates, the gnawing anxiety within him grew stronger and stronger. I can't take this much longer, he thought, his fingers itching to reach into his pocket and check his phone.

"Excuse me, do you have any ketchup?" a customer interrupted his thoughts, snapping him back to reality. Dean quickly grabbed a bottle from the condiment tray and handed it over with a strained smile that did little to hide his inner turmoil.

"Here you go, sir. Enjoy your meal," he said, his voice tight with tension.

"Thanks," the man replied obliviously, digging into his food.

As Dean turned away, he bit down hard on his lip, tasting the metallic tang of blood in his mouth. His mind raced with worst-case scenarios: Was one of his roommates hurt? Were they going to lose their apartment? But he shook off the dark thoughts, determined not to let them consume him.

No, everything will be fine, he told himself firmly. It has to be.

But despite his attempts at reassurance, the nagging feeling of uncertainty persisted, refusing to let him forget about the one call he couldn't bring himself to make - not yet, at least. As the hours dragged on and his break still seemed so far away, the constant pull of his buzzing phone in his pocket reminded him of the unknown awaiting him.

Dean's heart raced as he frantically scrolled through his phone, the dim glow of the screen casting eerie shadows across his face. He was hiding in a dark corner of the bustling dining area, trying to escape the chaos of the kitchen and find some comfort in his messages. But instead, each notification only added to the weight of worry that seemed to crush him.

"Hey, what's with the phone?" a gruff voice suddenly interrupted Dean's thoughts, causing him to jump and hide the device behind his back. The manager's stern expression caught him off guard, and he could feel his guilt rising like bile in his throat.

"You know the rules, Winchester," the manager scolded, his tone sharp and disapproving.

"I know. I'm sorry," Dean replied sheepishly, forcing a

smile while beads of sweat formed on his brow. "It won't happen again."

"It better not," the manager said skeptically before turning away to bark orders at another employee. Dean exhaled in relief and made a mental note to be more careful.

Dean tried to focus on his work in the restaurant, but his hands trembled slightly as he wiped down tables and refilled water glasses. Unanswered questions consumed his mind, each nagging at him like an unscratchable itch.

Why is this message so urgent? What could be so important right now? Dean couldn't shake off the situation's urgency despite trying to push it aside and concentrate on his job.

"Dean, can you take this to table seven?" a co-worker interrupted, handing him a plate with a forced smile that didn't quite reach their eyes. Dean forced himself to appear composed as he took the plate and headed towards the table, but inside, he felt like he was unraveling.

As he continued with his duties, the words of that urgent message echoed in his mind like a broken record, taunting him with all that remained unresolved.

"Please call us now" – the phrase repeatedly in his head, tempting him to sneak away and make the call. But he knew he couldn't risk getting into more trouble.

Taking a deep breath, Dean fought against his overwhelming fear and continued to work, determined not to let it consume him. But with each passing moment, the urge to make that call grew stronger, threatening to push him over the edge.

The clinking of silverware and the murmur of conversations filled the air, but it was all white noise for Dean. He mechanically cleared another table, his mind consumed with racing thoughts and a gnawing feeling in the pit of his stomach. The once comforting haven of the dimly lit restaurant now felt oppressive and suffocating.

"Hey, Dean," said Sarah, one of the waitresses, approaching with a tray full of empty glasses. "You alright? You seem off today."

He forced a smile, trying to keep up his usual cheerful facade. "Yeah, just got a lot on my mind."

Sarah rolled her eyes playfully. "Join the club, Winchester."

A brief moment of laughter from Sarah brought temporary relief before Dean's worries came crashing back. He couldn't shake the nagging feeling that something was wrong or the weight of impending doom settling in his chest.

As he refilled water glasses at the bar, he couldn't help but steal glances at the clock. Time, he seemed to move too fast and too slow, leaving him in limbo. What could be so urgent that it couldn't wait until after work? The unknown loomed over every passing minute like a dark cloud.

"Table eight needs clearing, Dean," said Marco, breaking through his thoughts.

With each step towards the table, dread settled heavier upon Dean's shoulders. "Please call us now" – the words he repeated like a haunting mantra. He couldn't ignore them anymore; he had to know what was happening.

"Hey, Marco," Dean said urgently, wiping down table eight. "I need to step out for a minute. It's urgent. Can you cover for me?"

Marco looked at him skeptically but nodded in understanding. "Sure, man, just make it quick."

Dean thanked him quickly before slipping out into the alley behind the restaurant. The cool air did little to calm the storm within him as he dialed his roommate's number. He desperately needed answers to ease his growing fears as no one answered their phones.

Dean was now feeling more restless and worried about his roommates. Despite his best efforts to focus on his work, he wiped down a table with practiced efficiency and whispered, "Keep it together, Dean. Just get through this shift, and then you can discover what's happening." He knew he had to stay focused and push through the anxiety until he could figure out what was happening with his friends.

Dean's aspirations of making a name for himself in the music industry slowly took over his thoughts as he continued to work as a busboy. After a long day of cleaning tables and carrying plates, he would often find comfort in the soothing sounds of his guitar, which provided a temporary escape from the mundanity of his daily routine. However, at this moment, as he navigated through the hustle and bustle of the kitchen, he couldn't help but feel a sense of unease about his prospects.

The weight of uncertainty and doubt was taking a toll on him, and he felt himself clenching his jaw as he tried to push these thoughts aside. Despite his passion for music, he knew he had to focus on his current job and not let his dreams distract him from his responsibilities. "Stay focused," he reminded himself. "You'll get your break soon enough, but for now, you've got to keep it together and stay on track."

The heavy wooden doors of the restaurant creaked open, releasing a burst of chilly air that raced through the room, causing a shiver to run down Rose Evan's spine. She was immediately engulfed in a bustling and lively scene as she crossed the threshold. The waitstaff weaved through the tables, gracefully balancing trays of delicious-looking dishes and refreshing beverages. At the same time, the din of happy patrons filled the air, creating an energetic symphony that quickened her heartbeat.

Rose took a deep breath and prepared herself for her first day as a hostess. She smoothed out her sleek, black uniform and adjusted the collar, glancing at her reflection in a nearby mirror. Despite appearing composed and mature for her 25 years, her eyes betrayed the bundle of nerves Rose was feeling. She retook another moment to adjust to the chaos before straightening her black hostess uniform again and steeling herself for her first day on the job. "Okay, Rose," she whispered to herself. "You can do this."

As an empathetic individual, she often felt others' emotions deeply, almost overwhelmingly. But today, she was determined to harness this empathy to excel in her new role and demonstrate her ability to navigate any challenge that came her way.

Rose was lost in her thoughts, trying to devise a plan to pay some bills, when she was suddenly jolted back to reality by an impatient voice. A woman was standing before her, tapping her foot and irritated.

"Excuse me!" A sharp voice interrupted her thoughts, causing her to turn and face a woman tapping her foot impatiently. "We've been waiting for a table."

"Oh, I'm so sorry," Rose stammered, striving to maintain her composure as she swiftly grabbed a stack of menus and led the customer to a vacant spot by the window. "Here you go, ma'am. Your server will be right with you."

"Finally," the woman huffed, rolling her eyes as she settled into the booth.

"Thank you for your patience," Rose managed to say, forcing a smile despite the knot of nerves in her stomach. She understood that not every customer would be understanding or kind, but she refused to let their impatience affect her performance.

Returning to the hostess stand, Rose glanced at Dean, who efficiently cleared a nearby table. He was deep in thought and had a tense expression. She longed to comfort him for some reason but knew she had her battles to conquer.

"First-day jitters?" A fellow hostess noticed Rose's anxious demeanor and offered a warm smile. "Don't worry; it gets easier."

"Thank you," Rose replied gratefully, absorbing the encouragement. "I'm just trying to get the hang of things."

"Remember, you've got this," the co-worker reassured her with a smile. "And hey, on the bright side, don't forget – we get a free meal each shift."

"Really? That's incredibly generous!" Rose's face lit up at the thought of a complimentary meal, her eagerness to learn and adapt shining through. Every little bit would help as she navigated this new chapter in her life.

"Absolutely," the other hostess confirmed with a nod. "Just make sure you put your order in during a lull in the rush."

"I will," Rose vowed, feeling renewed determination with the support of her colleague.

Amidst the hustle and bustle of the lunch hour, Rose effortlessly managed her hostess duties at the restaurant. She skillfully accommodated customers' requests and ensured the smooth traffic flow in the dining area. Despite her challenges, Rose remained determined to make a positive impact on herself and everyone who walked through the door.

While she worked tirelessly, the weight of her emotions was palpable, but she persevered, driven by her desire to succeed. Amid the chaos, Rose hoped to find her place in this world, to carve out a space where she could thrive and make a difference.

As Dean walked through the busy kitchen, he couldn't help but feel overwhelmed by the noise. The sound of rattling plates and clanging utensils filled the air, mixed with the sizzle of hot pans, creating an almost deafening cacophony. He carefully balanced a tray of dirty dishes in his arms, trying to avoid bumping into any of his colleagues who were rushing past him.

With his head on a swivel, Dean scanned the room, his eyes searching for an open spot at the dishwasher. That's when he caught sight of Rose, one of the new hires, looking around with wide, curious eyes. Even amidst the chaos, their eyes met briefly, and Dean couldn't help but feel a sense of intrigue pass between them as if they were sharing a secret amid the whirlwind around them.

Dean pushed through the crowded kitchen, trying to avoid the chaotic flurry of activity around him. He muttered, "Excuse me," under his breath as he deftly dodged a cook carrying a steaming pot. The brief connection with Rose had momentarily distracted him from his task. He had dirty dishes he was carrying to their rightful places, and time was running out.

His phone buzzed incessantly in his pocket, demanding his attention and adding to his growing sense of urgency. Dean knew he couldn't afford any delays. He needed to focus all his energy on getting the dishes cleaned and returned as quickly as possible and make it in time to attend to the demands of his buzzing phone.

Amid a bustling restaurant, Dean called out to a nearby waiter, his eyes fixed on the precarious stack of plates before him. Dean focused intently on his task, his hands deftly maneuvering the dishes as he weaved through a maze of busy waitstaff, narrowly avoiding collisions. Despite the chaos around him, his dedication to his work was unwavering, and his skill and precision were evident in every movement.

As he made his way towards his destination, his mind was plagued by a constant stream of worries - thoughts of a possible eviction and the weight of his beloved guitar, which he knew he could not afford to replace if anything were to happen to it. Still, he soldiered on, driven by a fierce determination to succeed and a deep love for his craft.

*What could be happening at the apartment right now? * He wondered, fighting to recheck his phone. *I can't let this affect my performance here. I need this job more than ever. *

A voice cut through the bustling restaurant, demanding Dean's attention. "Dean! Table six needs clearing!" he heard, jolting him out of his thoughts. He quickly nodded in acknowledgment, placing the dishes he had been holding onto a nearby table before hurrying towards the direction of table six.

Despite his personal life being heavy on his mind, he refused to let it affect his work. He prided himself on being a reliable and efficient staff member and wouldn't let anything get in the way of that.

As he drew closer to table six, Dean's gaze flickered towards Rose, who was now conversing with a customer. He couldn't help but admire her composure and determination, especially on her first work day.

Her eyes sparkled fiercely, reflecting her unwavering dedication to her job. Despite the chaos around them, Rose seemed to be in her element, efficiently handling the situation. As he reached the table, Dean couldn't help but feel a sense of pride for his colleague.

A man offered a small smile as he reached to hand her back the menu. "Here you go," he said in a gentle tone. Rose, a hostess, received the menu with a grateful expression. She had been feeling a bit flustered with the busy lunchtime rush, but the man's gesture of kindness helped ease her nerves.

"You're doing great," he added, and Rose felt a surge of confidence wash over her. She returned his smile with an appreciative nod and turned to her next customer with renewed vigor, ready to provide the same exceptional service that had earned her the man's praise.

Dean stood there, observing her intently for a while longer, studying her every move and sensing a deep familiarity in her unyielding strength and tenacity. As he went about his daily tasks, he couldn't help but harbor the notion that their paths would keep crossing, that their fates were intertwined in ways they were yet to fathom.

However, for now, he had a job to do - and so did she. Individually, they confronted the pandemonium head-on, each with a firm resolve to surmount their hurdles and possibly emerge stronger on the other side amid the chaos.

After finishing her duties, Rose returned to the hostess stand. As she walked, she couldn't help but feel a little overwhelmed by the busy atmosphere of the restaurant. However, her attention was soon caught by her colleague, Melissa, who was waving her over from across the room.

Melissa had been working at the restaurant for a few months and quickly became one of the most reliable and efficient hostesses on staff. Rose felt curious and admired as she approached Melissa, hoping to learn from her experience and expertise. Despite the chaos and commotion surrounding them, Rose couldn't help but feel a sense of calm and reassurance in Melissa's presence.

"Hey, Rose! You seem to be holding up pretty well on your first day," Melissa said with a friendly smile.

"Thanks, but it's been a bit overwhelming at times," Rose admitted, tucking a stray strand of hair behind her ear. "I'm trying my best, though."

"Trust me, we all felt like that on our first day," Melissa assured her. "But you'll get the hang of it soon enough. Just remember to stay calm and focused when dealing with demanding customers. They can smell fear," she added with a wink.

"Right," Rose nodded, taking in the advice. "Stay calm and focused. I'll try to remember that."

"And don't forget," Melissa continued, "did anyone tell you about your free meal each day you work? It's just one of the perks of working here."

"Really?" Rose's eyes lit up at the news. "That's amazing. Someone might have mentioned it, but there's so much going on! Thank you so much for telling me, too." Her gratitude shone through her words, making it clear that she was eager to learn and grow in her new environment.

"Of course," Melissa replied. "Now, go out there and show those customers what you're made of!"

Rose sat attentively, listening to the advice and encouragement she was being given. Meanwhile, Dean was occupied with clearing tables in the busy diner. Dean's mind was preoccupied with the text message he had received earlier.

As he meticulously wiped down the remnants of another customer's meal, he couldn't help but allow his thoughts to drift back to the message and its implications. His composure wavered as he struggled to process the information and its potential impact on his life.

"Dean!" His manager's voice cut through his thoughts like a knife, jolting him back to reality. "You're taking too long to clear these tables. We need them ready for the next customers!"

"Sorry, sir," Dean replied quickly, his face flushing with embarrassment. He felt a knot tighten in his chest as he realized that his preoccupation had affected his work performance. Determined to make up for lost time, he doubled his efforts, expertly balancing trays and plates as he moved through the crowded kitchen with newfound urgency.

As he navigated the chaos, Dean glanced over at Rose, who was now confidently greeting another group of customers. Despite the whirlwind of emotions inside him, a small smile tugged at the corners of his mouth. He admired her ability to adapt quickly and silently rooted for her success.

Dean had been having a tough day at work, feeling like he was falling behind and not meeting his manager's expectations. But he wasn't one to give up easily. With renewed determination, Dean set out to prove himself and salvage what was left of his shift. He knew the only way to overcome life's obstacles was to face them head-on, just like his friend Rose did. Dean seemed to admire her for the resilience and strength he saw.

Despite his challenges, Dean felt a spark of creativity igniting within him. He was an artist, and even during the most challenging times, he never stopped dreaming.

As he worked, he started to see ways to turn the situation around, using his skills and ingenuity to make something great out of a challenging situation.

Rose stood at the hostess stand, her fingers tracing the polished wood as she braced herself for the onslaught of customers. A group of six walked in, their voices loud and demanding even before they reached her.

"Excuse me, we had a reservation for six, but now there are eight of us," said a tall man with slicked-back hair, not bothering to hide his impatience. "And we need a table closer to the window."

"Of course, sir," Rose replied, swallowing her nerves and forcing a smile. "Let me check our availability."

As she scanned the floor plan, her mind raced with what her fellow hostess had told her earlier. This was her chance to prove herself. Taking a deep breath, she found a suitable table and made the necessary adjustments.

"Alright, we can accommodate your group," Rose said, her voice steadier than before. "Please follow me."

As she led the group through the bustling restaurant, she couldn't help but feel overwhelmed by the weight of their expectations. It seemed like everyone was watching her, waiting for her to make a mistake. But she refused to let them see her falter.

Dean's heart raced as he quietly slipped into the back

of the kitchen, his eyes darting around in search of his manager. He was on edge, nervous about being caught in an unauthorized area. After a quick scan of the room, he found a secluded corner and reached for his phone, eager to check for any updates from his roommates.

As he unlocked his device, his screen was instantly flooded with missed calls and frantic text messages, each one more urgent and concerning than the last. Dean's anxiety spiked as he read through them, wondering what could have possibly happened while he was at work.

Dean was at his wit's end and couldn't bear the situation any longer. Frustrated and anxious, he took a deep breath and hit the call button on his phone. As the phone rang, he held his breath, waiting for one of his roommates to answer. Finally, one of them picked up and, with a rush of words, spilled everything weighing on Dean's mind like an avalanche.

Dean's roommate trembled with fear as he said, "Dean, you must come here right now! The Sheriff is at our doorstep, and he's threatening to evict us from the apartment. He says he'll throw all our belongings on the street if we don't leave immediately. We need to figure out what to do, and fast!"

Dean let out a curse word in a low voice, feeling his chest tighten with anxiety as he almost dropped his phone. Dean started talking again to his roommate, and the urgency in his voice was evident as he spoke. "Please, I need you to take care of something for me. My guitar is in my room. Can you make sure it's safe? It means a lot to me, and I don't want anything to happen to it."

His roommate mumbled a response, but the uncertainty in his voice did little to ease Dean's worries. He hoped he could trust his friend to keep his beloved instrument out of harm's way.

Dean allowed himself to process the situation as he hung up the call. His world was crumbling around him, and yet he had no choice but to continue working, to put on the mask of the ever-reliable busboy. He took a deep breath before returning to face the restaurant floor's chaos.

Back at the hostess stand, Rose felt relief wash over her as the group she helped settled into their table without further issues. She knew that this was only the beginning, that there would be countless more challenges ahead—but maybe, just maybe, she could handle them.

Rose leaned against the hostess stand, her breaths coming in shallow gasps as she tried to regain her composure. The noise of chattering customers and clinking silverware filled the air, but it was as if she stood alone amidst the whirlwind of activity for a moment.

She hadn't realized she was holding her breath until she

caught sight of Dean across the room. He seemed lost in thought, his eyes filled with worry. She couldn't help but wonder what could be troubling him amidst the chaos. Their eyes briefly met, and Rose felt a strange connection for a fleeting moment before quickly looking away, feeling a warmth rise to her cheeks.

Dean's thoughts were consumed by the conversation with his roommate, sending waves of panic surging through him. He tried to shake it off, knowing he had a job, but the image of his beloved guitar left out on the street haunted him. He couldn't afford to lose it—not when music was the one thing keeping him afloat amid life's struggles.

"Hey, are you okay?" one of his co-workers asked, nudging him gently.

"Uh, yeah," Dean lied, forcing a smile onto his face. "Just got some bad news, is all."

"Sorry to hear that, man," the co-worker replied sympathetically, clapping him on the back. "Hang in there."

Dean nodded, taking a deep breath, watching Rose bustling around the hostess stand. Something about her—an air of determination and vulnerability—stirred something within him. As much as he wanted to reach out, share his troubles, or offer support, he knew now wasn't the time. They both had a job to do, their battles to fight.

"Thanks," Dean muttered, more to himself than anyone else. With renewed determination, he dove back into the fray, trying to focus on clearing tables and refilling glasses while his thoughts raced.

Rose glanced up again, catching a glimpse of Dean's retreating figure as he disappeared into the kitchen. Something inside her fluttered, a sense of anticipation mingling with concern. Though they barely spoke, she felt a connection between them—an unspoken understanding that life had thrown them both curveballs. And even though they were in the throes of their storms, there was a glimmer of hope that together, perhaps they could weather whatever came their way.

Rose's weary eyes blinked against the bright overhead lights as she glanced at the clock, noticing her lunch break was fast approaching. Her stomach growled softly, a reminder that she hadn't eaten all day—a testament to the whirlwind of emotions and tasks that had consumed her.

"Hey, Rose," the fellow hostess said, noticing her apprehension. "Remember, you get a free meal each shift. Just order something from the kitchen."

"Right, thank you," she replied with a shaky smile, grateful for the unexpected kindness.

As she hesitantly approached the kitchen window, she

felt a sudden jolt of nerves. The chefs were busy at work, their movements precise and swift like a well-rehearsed dance. She wondered if she would ever feel that comfortable in this chaotic environment.

"Um, excuse me?" Rose called out timidly, catching the attention of one of the chefs. "Could I please have a turkey sandwich?"

"Of course," he replied with a friendly nod, quickly assembling the sandwich and handing it to her.

"Thank you," she murmured, feeling more at ease.

Securing her meal, Rose slipped past the bustling waitstaff and approached the exit. As she did so, she unknowingly crossed paths with Dean again. Their eyes met briefly, each acknowledging the other's presence amidst the chaos. Rose noticed the frustration across his face, an emotion she could relate to all too well.

"Everything okay?" she asked, concern lacing her voice.

"Uh, yeah. It's just personal stuff," Dean admitted, trying to brush off his worries. I'm heading out for my lunch break; I need some fresh air."

"Same here," Rose said, offering a tentative smile. "I have to run this meal home first to my boyfriend, and then maybe we could hang out during the rest of our break?"

Dean hesitated, his mind still reeling from the devastating news about his home. But something about Rose—a sense of understanding and empathy—comforted him.

"Sure," he agreed, his voice softening. "I could use the company."

Chapter 2

With his back against the rough, weather-worn brick wall, Dean Winchester held his beloved guitar with great care. Its glossy, polished wood gleamed with the intricate patterns of the fretboard and the strings glinting in its shadows. Knowing how much it meant to him, his roommates had thoughtfully brought it to him during his break.

Dean ran his fingers over the strings, feeling the familiar grooves of the fretboard under his touch. He strummed a few chords, the guitar echoing softly in the alley. The music was soothing, bringing a sense of calm to his frayed nerves. As he played, he closed his eyes and lost himself in the music, letting the guitar's notes carry him away.

"Thanks for bringing this," he said, smiling at his roommates. "I needed it."

"Of course, man," replied Jake, one of his oldest friends and bandmates. They exchanged glances with the unspoken understanding that music was their shared lifeline.

Dean furrowed his brow and cleared his throat, trying to shift the attention back to the pressing matter at hand. "Alright, what will we do about this eviction?" he asked, his voice laced with concern. He stared at each of their faces, hoping for an answer from one of them. But as the silence stretched on, he could feel the weight of their collective gaze bearing down on him. He knew they were all waiting for him to speak up and solve the problem.

But the truth was that he was just as stumped as they were. His mind raced as he tried to devise a plan, but nothing seemed to stick. He took a deep breath, trying to steady himself, and focused again on the group, hoping that someone would have something to contribute.

With a tone that conveyed a sense of urgency and desperation, he implored his companions, "Please, let's put our heads together and devise a plan. We can't just sit back and let them evict us onto the streets. We need to figure something out and fast." His voice quivered slightly, betraying the fear and anxiety that he was feeling at that moment.

His roommates exchanged glances, the weight of their situation sinking in. It wasn't just about losing a place to live—it was about losing the home where they'd built their dreams together—the place where they'd practiced late into the night, pouring their hearts and souls into their music.

"Dean," Jake began hesitantly, "I think... I think we've all figured out where we're going next."

"Really? That's great!" Dean exclaimed, hope blossoming in his chest. "What's the plan?"

"Well, uh..." Jake rubbed the back of his neck, avoiding eye contact. "We're all going back to our parents' places."

Dean was caught off-guard by the sudden realization that he was alone in the cold. The words hit him like a punch to the gut, leaving him more vulnerable than ever. He couldn't help but think about the fact that he didn't have the luxury of calling his parents for comfort, as they had passed away long ago.

The band had been his family, rock, and support system through thick and thin. But now, as he stood there alone, a bitter taste filled his mouth, and he couldn't shake off the feeling of loneliness and despair that had taken hold of him.

"Right," he said quietly, trying to hide the hurt in his voice. "I guess that makes sense."

"Hey, man, we're sorry," Jake offered, placing a hand on Dean's shoulder. "We'd help if we could, but..."

"Save it," Dean interrupted, forcing a smile. "It's not your fault. I'll figure something out."

As his roommates stood before him, they all wore a look of guilt that stubbornly refused to leave their faces. They nodded in acknowledgment of the situation they had created and murmured their goodbyes before turning around and walking away.

He was alone in the alley, with only his guitar for some company and the sun slowly sinking in the sky, casting a warm, orange glow over everything around him. Despite the peacefulness of the moment, he couldn't help but feel a sense of loneliness wash over him as he stood there, taking in the sights and sounds of the city around him.

As the last rays of light faded, so did Dean's hope. He had yet to learn where he would go or what he would do. But he couldn't let his dreams slip away without a fight.

The guitar's weight in his hands felt heavier than usual as if it were an anchor tying him to the fading light of his dreams. Dean's fingers traced the familiar grooves on the instrument, seeking solace in its worn wood. He could feel the panic rising like a tidal wave threatening to wash away everything he had worked for.

"Dean?" Lisa, the youngest member of their band, asked hesitantly. "Are you okay?"

"Sure," Dean lied, forcing a laugh that sounded strangled even to him. "Just trying to figure out my next move."

"Hey, we're sorry about all this," Chris piped up, his voice thick with guilt. "We don't want to leave you hanging."

"Guys, I get it," Dean assured them, swallowing hard against the lump in his throat. "You've got your safety nets, and that's great. Really. I'll find a way to make things work."

"Promise you won't give up on music?" Lisa asked, her eyes pleading with him not to abandon their shared passion.

"Promise," Dean replied, the word tasting like a vow and a prayer.

As they turned to leave, Dean couldn't help but watch their retreating figures with a sense of loss. They were moving on, and he was left in the debris of their shattered dreams. He paced back and forth outside the restaurant, his mind racing as though it could outrun the impending eviction.

"Homeless," he muttered under his breath, the word echoing in his ears like a death knell. The thought sent a shiver down his spine – a chilling reminder of how quickly everything could be snatched away from him.

"Okay, Dean, think," he urged himself, clenching his fists in determination. "There's always a way. There has to be."

His heart hammered against his chest, each beat reminding him of the ticking clock that was his life. Time was running out, and Dean knew he couldn't afford to waste more of it.

The first cold gust of wind brushed Dean's face like a cruel reminder of the uncertainty ahead. He felt an unspoken hurt gnawing at his heart, knowing that his band had deserted him forever and all of his musical dreams with them.

"Hey, man," said a fellow busboy as he passed. "You, okay?"

"Yeah," Dean replied, forcing a smile to mask the pain that threatened to spill over. "Just needed some fresh air."

His thoughts were filled with overwhelming despair as he gazed at the darkening sky. The vast clouds above seemed to reflect the turmoil within his mind, and he yearned for a way to escape the harsh reality that weighed him down.

With a deep longing, he wished to sprout wings and soar into the unknown, leaving behind the daily troubles that plagued him. The gentle breeze that stirred the trees around him only intensified his yearning as he felt the weight of his sorrows pressing down upon him with unrelenting force.

"Alright, dude. See you inside," the busboy said, patting Dean on the back before heading into the restaurant.

"See you," Dean replied, his voice barely audible.

Taking a deep breath, he closed his eyes and let his imagination wander. The images that unfolded were a stark contrast to the tranquility he sought. He saw their belongings – guitars, amps, clothing – strewn across the street like casualties of war, torn apart and discarded without a second thought. He envisioned himself scrambling to collect the remnants of their life together, his fingers numb from the cold and heart heavy with defeat.

"Enough," he whispered, shaking his head to banish the haunting visions. With every step he took toward the restaurant, he felt the weight of his future pressing down upon him.

"Dean!" called out his manager from behind the counter as he entered, oblivious to the storm brewing within him. "You're back! We're getting slammed out there."

"Got it, boss," Dean said, nodding with determination.

He knew now was not the time to wallow in despair; he had a job and responsibilities to uphold.

He approached his locker with care and tenderness, gently turning the lock to reveal its contents. His most prized possession, a beautiful guitar, lay nestled inside, its strings glinting in the light. He paused momentarily, admiring the instrument's sleek curves and graceful lines, before carefully lifting it and cradling it in his arms.

As he placed it back in the locker, he took a moment to adjust its position, ensuring that it was protected from the harsh realities of the outside world. He gazed at the guitar for a moment longer, lost in thought, before closing the locker door with a soft click and turning to face the day ahead.

"Alright, Dean," he whispered, steeling his resolve. "You've got this. No matter what happens, you'll find a way."

With that, he turned on his heel, ready to face the challenges ahead. As he waded through the restaurant's chaos, he held onto the hope that, somehow, he would keep his promise to his bandmates and himself. Music was his life, and he wouldn't let it slip away without a fight.

Dean went through the crowded restaurant, balancing trays filled with food and drinks. He couldn't help but notice the chaotic noise surrounding him. The clinking of glasses, the sound of utensils hitting plates, and the boisterous laughter of the diners all blended to create a cacophonous symphony.

Despite the hustle and bustle of the busy restaurant, Dean felt isolated entirely in his world of emotions. It seemed like everyone around him was immune to the storm of feelings brewing inside him, leaving him to struggle alone.

"Hey, Lena," Dean said, flashing a warm smile at one of the waitresses as he unloaded the dirty dishes onto the counter. "How's your night going?"

"Ugh, don't even ask," she replied with an exaggerated roll of her eyes. "I swear, people must think we're magicians or something. Can't they see how busy we are?"

"Tell me about it," Dean chuckled, his mind racing with thoughts of eviction notices and abandoned dreams. He didn't want to burden Lena or anyone else with the weight on his shoulders. He'd always been the rock for those around him, and he refused to let that change now.

"Dean, table seven needs a clean-up," his manager called out from behind the cash register, snapping him back to reality.

"Got it, boss," he replied, nodding with determination. As he grabbed a rag and spray bottle, a melody began to form in his head – a defiant anthem that seemed to rise above the noise and chaos, reminding him of who he was and what he stood for.

"Excuse me," Dean said politely as he sidestepped a group of customers and made his way to the messy table. The scent of forgotten meals lingered in the air, but it couldn't drown out the music that now echoed within him.

"Hey, Dean," chimed in another coworker, Mark, as they worked side by side to clear the mess. "You seem pretty cheerful tonight, considering how slammed we are."

"Music keeps me going, man," Dean admitted, a genuine smile gracing his lips. "No matter what happens, I can always count on a good song to lift me."

"Music, huh?" Mark mused, nodding in understanding. "I guess we all have ways of coping with the madness."

"Definitely," Dean agreed, his thoughts drifting to the uncertain road ahead. He knew that the journey wouldn't be easy, but he also knew that as long as he had music by his side, he could face whatever challenges life threw at him.

"Hey, guys," Lena called out as she approached the two busboys, her arms laden with yet another stack of dirty dishes. "Would you Mind giving me a hand?"

"Of course," Dean said, reaching out to take the load from her, his smile never wavering. "We're all in this together, right?"

"Right," Lena agreed, returning his smile with her own. As they stood there, surrounded by the whirlwind of activity and the symphony of clattering plates, Dean felt a renewed sense of purpose—a determination to survive and thrive, no matter what the future held.

The soft flicker of candlelight danced across the restaurant walls, casting a warm glow over the bustling scene. Servers weaved their way through tables, delivering steaming plates of food to eager customers as laughter and conversation filled the air. Amidst the chaos, Dean moved with purpose, his eyes scanning the room for any dishes needing clearing or guests needing assistance.

"Hey, Dean, can you grab those plates from table six?" said Samantha, one of the waitresses. She was juggling orders, trying not to spill the glasses of wine on her tray.

"Sure thing, Sam," Dean replied, maintaining his cheerful demeanor despite his turmoil. He swiftly collected the dirty dishes, stacking them with expert precision before returning to the kitchen. As he passed by his manager, Helen, he nodded in acknowledgment, receiving a grateful smile.

"Keep up the good work, Dean," she said, her voice barely audible over the restaurant's din. "We're swamped tonight."

"I will do that, Helen," he responded, forcing a grin that

belied his panic. The eviction notice burned in his pocket, a constant reminder of the uncertainty looming ahead. Yet he couldn't let it consume him, not while he still had a job to do and responsibilities to uphold.

"Dean, can you help me out here?" asked Mike, another busboy, gesturing towards a recently vacated table laden with empty plates and crumpled napkins. "I've got my hands full with this one."

"Of course," Dean said, his thoughts momentarily pushed aside as he focused on the task. Together, they cleared the table, working in tandem like a well-oiled machine.

"Thanks, man," Mike said, wiping the sweat from his brow. "It's crazy tonight."

"Tell me about it," Dean muttered, his mind racing with the weight of his predicament. How would he find a new place to live on such short notice? And what about his music? With his bandmates returning home, he felt like the rug had been pulled out from under him. But he couldn't dwell on it now – not when work would still be done.

"Hey, are you okay?" Mike asked, noticing the fleeting look of anguish on Dean's face.

"Yeah, I'm good," Dean replied quickly, forcing another smile. "Just thinking about how much I need a coffee break."

"Same here," Mike said with a chuckle, clapping Dean on the back. "Let's grab one after our shifts, huh?"

"Sounds like a plan," Dean agreed, his heart aching at the thought of losing his home and the camaraderie he'd built with his coworkers. He took a deep breath, steeling himself for the remainder of the night, determined not to let his struggles interfere with his job.

Dean's mind was a whirlwind of emotions and uncertainty as he continued to clear tables and assist customers. Yet he held onto a glimmer of hope, the unwavering belief that he would find a way to overcome these challenges and pursue his passion for music, no matter the obstacles ahead. The road may have been uncertain, but Dean Winchester was nothing if not resilient.

Even though sadness was casting a long shadow across the dimly lit restaurant floor, despite the weight of his worries, Dean continued to work with an impressive fervor, clearing tables and filling water glasses with a practiced hand.

"Dean," a waitress named Emily approached him. Her brow furrowed in concern. "You've been quiet tonight. Is everything okay?"

For a moment, Dean hesitated, debating whether or not to share the burden of his thoughts. But as much as he wanted to unload, he couldn't bring himself to worry her.

Instead, he smiled—a genuine one this time—and said, "I'm fine, Emily. I'm just thinking about some stuff, that's all. You know, band things."

"Ah," she nodded understandingly. "How are they doing, by the way? Your bandmates, I mean."

His heart clenched at the mention of them, but he forced himself to maintain his composure. "They're good. Everyone's just trying to figure out their next steps, you know? But I have faith in them. We'll find our way back together eventually."

"Sounds like you care about them," Emily remarked, touched by his unwavering loyalty.

"Of course. They're my family, you know? And music... well, it's everything to me," he admitted, his eyes shining with determination.

As she looked at him with earnest eyes, she squeezed his hand reassuringly and said, "Your passion for music is truly inspiring, Dean. I doubt you'll make it big with your talent and hard work someday. It may seem tough sometimes, but please don't give up on your dreams, alright? Keep pushing forward and chasing after what you truly desire."

"Thanks, Emily," he replied, grateful for her encouragement. "I won't."

With renewed resolve, Dean refocused on his tasks, his mind racing to find a new place to live and a way to keep pursuing his passion for music. The road ahead may have been uncertain, but Dean Winchester was nothing if not determined, and he would face challenges with unwavering dedication.

Chapter 3

As Rose returned to the restaurant from her lunch break, the golden light emanating from the chandeliers cast a warm glow on the polished door handles through which she entered. However, the shadows on her face seemed to deepen, almost like they were dancing slowly, adding a mysterious aura to her already enigmatic personality. Dean felt a sudden urge to check his phone as she walked in, reminding him of the time when he had to secretly hide it from their manager, sparking a wave of anxiety within him.

As he continued to observe her throughout the day, he couldn't help but notice that something seemed off. During her lunch break, she took too long to return on her first day, causing him to feel slightly concerned. Her usual warmth and friendliness had vanished, replaced by a distant and reserved demeanor. He found himself wondering what could have happened to cause such a shift in her behavior and how he could help her feel more at ease once again.

Dean raised his voice to catch her attention as Rose walked towards him. He tried to sound calm, but his tone had an underlying sense of worry. "Hey, Rose, is everything alright?" he asked, his eyes scanning her face for any signs of distress. He wanted to ensure she was okay and offer support if needed.

When asked how she was doing, she smiled half-heartedly, "I'm fine." Despite her efforts to conceal her true feelings, her voice quivered slightly, indicating that she struggled to control her emotions. She was going through a tough time, and her response was just a way of avoiding further discussion about her situation.

Dean watched her closely as she busied herself tending to the customers, her every movement calculated and precise. He could see the strain etched across her delicate features, the way her hands shook ever so slightly as she handed out menus or retrieved empty plates. It was like a storm brewing beneath the surface, threatening to erupt at any moment.

Dean gently grabbed Rose's arm as she walked past him, offering a kind smile. "Hey, Rose," he whispered, his voice barely above a murmur. "I just wanted to let you know that you can always talk to me, okay? We're friends, and I care. I'm here to listen if there's anything on your mind."

"Dean, I'm okay," she insisted, pulling her arm away gently but firmly. Her eyes darted around the room, ensuring no one noticed their conversation. "I just...have a lot on my mind, that's all."

"Is it your boyfriend?" Dean asked hesitantly, immediately regretting the question as Rose's eyes widened in shock. "Sorry, I didn't mean to pry," he quickly added, backtracking.

"No, it's not your fault," she assured him, her gaze clouded with pain. "Just...not here, okay? I can't talk about it here."

"Of course," Dean agreed, nodding understandingly. He watched Rose walk away, each step weighing her down further into the depths of her despair. All he wanted was to help her, but how could he when she wouldn't let him in?

As Dean cleared away the remnants of another table's meal, he couldn't help but feel relief that Rose hadn't been there to witness his band's disintegration earlier. At least they both had one less thing to worry about, but as the hours wore on and the restaurant slowly emptied, he couldn't shake the feeling that something needed to be done to help Rose face whatever demons were haunting her.

He hoped he would find the strength before it was too late.

Seated at a back table, Rose's fingers trembled as she meticulously folded napkins into delicate fans. The memories of her lunch break haunted her, playing out like a cruel film reel in her mind. Her heart shattered into a thousand pieces when she opened her apartment door.

Dominic's voice rang out through the room, "Surprise!" as he playfully tugged at the hem of the other woman's shirt. Rose's heart sank as she stood frozen in the doorway, her eyes widening with shock at the sight before her. Her hand, clutching a bag of food, suddenly went numb, and the bag slipped from her grasp, crashing to the floor with a loud thud.

Lost in her thoughts, her mind raced with about a million of them, wondering how she could have been so blind to what was happening right under her nose. The silence in the room was deafening as the three exchanged uneasy glances, each uncertain how to break the tense silence.

Rose's world came crashing down around her as she stumbled backward, tears already blurring her vision. She couldn't believe what she had just heard - the man she loved, the one she had opened up to and trusted with everything, had betrayed her.

Fleeing to the bathroom, she slammed the door shut and locked it, her heart pounding so hard she thought it might burst through her chest. She leaned heavily against the sink, her knuckles white as she clutched the edge, trying to find some semblance of control amidst the chaos of her emotions.

Through the door, she could hear Dominic's frantic excuses, his words dripping with insincerity as he tried to justify his actions and convince her to open up. But Rose knew that nothing he could say would make this right. Not now, not ever.

"Rose, I swear it's not what it looks like! She's just... We were only... It doesn't mean anything!"

But even as he spoke, Rose knew that his words were hollow. He wasn't sorry for hurting her; he was sorry for getting caught. Her thoughts raced, an unbearable storm surging within her as she searched for something—anything—to alleviate the pain.

Frantically searching for relief, she quickly scanned the contents of the medicine cabinet until her eyes landed on a small bottle of pills.

The medication had been prescribed to her after a minor surgical procedure but had since been forgotten and left untouched on the shelf for months. As she reached for the bottle, her hand shook with hesitation.

She knew the potential risks of taking expired medication, but the pain was becoming unbearable. At that moment, her heart seemed to skip a beat as she considered whether the relief was worth the gamble.

Rose's frustration boiled over as she snatched the bottle from the medicine cabinet and hurriedly slipped it into her pocket. She gritted her teeth and stormed past Dominic without so much a glance, her eyes red-rimmed and brimming with tears that she could barely hold back. It was clear that something had deeply upset her, and her curt tone only confirmed it. "I have to get back to work," she snapped before disappearing.

"Rose, wait!" he called after her, but she refused to turn back. She slammed the door behind her, leaving him standing in their tainted home.

Rose returned to the restaurant with a heavy heart, feeling a sense of dread that seemed to hang over her like a dark cloud. She knew she had to focus on her work, so she took a deep breath and tried to push her worries aside. As she approached the table, she forced a smile and greeted the customers, doing her best to appear friendly and professional.

However, her mind was elsewhere. As she folded the napkins with meticulous precision from years of practice, she couldn't shake the unease that gnawed at her insides. In her pocket, she felt the weight of the pill bottle, a constant reminder of the decision she had yet to make. Should she take them? Should she not? The uncertainty was suffocating, and she couldn't help but wonder what the consequences of her choice would be.

As Rose stood in front of the bathroom mirror, she couldn't help but notice how pale her face looked. Her eyes were rimmed with red, and they shone with unshed tears. The pill bottle clutched tightly in her trembling hand was a stark reminder of the situation she found herself in. She stared at it, her eyes flickering with anger and desperation.

The pills inside seemed to mock her, daring her to make a decision that would change everything. The label on the bottle was clear as day, and she knew exactly what the pills were capable of. She took a deep breath to steady her nerves, but her hands only shook more. The bathroom silence was overwhelming, and she could only hear the faint hum of the fluorescent light above her.

She closed her eyes for a moment, trying to gather her thoughts, but the pills seemed to be calling out to her, urging her to take them. Every fiber of her being was telling her not to, but at the same time, she couldn't shake off the thought that maybe, just maybe, they would help her escape the pain that had been consuming her for days.

A voice suddenly interrupted her reverie as she stood there, lost in her dark thoughts. "Hey, are you okay?" The sound came from behind her, and she was immediately startled out of her brooding. She quickly reached into her pocket to conceal the bottle she had been clutching tightly. As she turned around, she saw one of her coworkers looking at her with a concerned expression. The crease on their forehead was a clear indication of their worry. Despite her initial surprise, she was grateful for their concern.

Rose put on a brave face and forced a shaky smile, trying to convince herself that everything was okay. "Yeah, I'm fine," she lied, hoping her coworker wouldn't notice the redness in her eyes and how her nose twitched. "It's just allergies, you know?" She tried to ignore the persistent itchiness in her throat and how her chest felt tight, but it was hard to mask her discomfort.

"Ah, those can be brutal. Hang in there," they said sympathetically before leaving the bathroom.

Rose glanced back at the mirror, her reflection staring

back at her accusingly, but she pushed the pills from her mind and focused on finishing her shift.

Meanwhile, Dean moved almost mechanically through the restaurant, his movements slow and deliberate as he cleared away dishes from empty tables. Thoughts of his band's breakup and the eviction notice weighed heavily on him, and the reality of his situation loomed large: he had nowhere to go once the restaurant closed for the night.

"Hey, Dean, you good?" a server asked as he passed by, noticing his unusually somber demeanor.

"Uh, yeah, just a lot on my mind," Dean replied, forcing a smile that didn't quite reach his eyes. "But don't worry about me; I'll be fine."

"Alright, man. If you need anything, let me know," the server said before disappearing back into the hustle and bustle of the restaurant.

Dean's eyes darted around the space, unconsciously searching for Rose. Where is she? he wondered, concern building within him. He'd noticed something was off when she returned from her break, and his protective part ached to help her, even if it meant momentarily setting aside his problems.

But for now, all he could do was continue clearing tables, each representing another step closer to facing the uncertainty of the night ahead.

The restaurant's once lively atmosphere was now muted, the last customer having left for the night. Dean and
Rose, both adrift in their separate sorrows, found themselves alone within the dimly lit building. The hushed
clink of glassware and the faint creaks of settling chairs
echoed through the space, a melancholy soundtrack to the
evening.

Rose, her heart heavy with betrayal, retreated to the
storage closet. She pressed her back against the wall and
slid down, pulling her knees close to her chest. A tear rolled
down her cheek as she stared blankly at the rows of neatly
stacked napkins, lost in thoughts of Dominic's infidelity
and the pills still tucked away in her pocket. Unbeknownst
to her, Dean's mind was similarly occupied with his struggles.

Outside, Dean leaned against the hood of his car, his
gaze fixed on the cityscape before him. The soft glow of
the streetlights cast shadows across his furrowed brow,
highlighting the worry etched into his features. He took a
deep breath, inhaling the scent of cooling asphalt mingled
with the tang of exhaust fumes. The city seemed so vast,
yet he couldn't help but feel confined by the weight of his
current reality.

"Damn," he muttered under his breath, letting his fingers drum idly against the car's metal surface. "What am I

gonna do now?"

At that moment, numbed by the prospect of losing everything he had worked so hard for, Dean allowed himself to imagine an alternate path. He envisioned himself playing sold-out shows, his guitar resonating with the chords of his dreams, each note echoing the passion that burned within him. He longed for a life where music coursed through his veins, propelling him toward a future filled with promise and possibility.

But just as quickly, the harsh truth of his situation snapped him back to reality. His band was no more, his home slipping away like sand between his fingers. As he stared out at the city, listening to the distant hum of traffic and the murmur of nighttime conversations, Dean couldn't help but wonder if his dreams were nothing more than a fleeting mirage.

"Maybe it's time to face the music," he whispered to himself, the irony of his words not lost on him. He shook his head, trying to dispel the lingering remnants of hope that clung stubbornly to his heart.

Inside, Rose inhaled shakily, her eyes brimming with unshed tears. She knew she had to confront her demons to find the strength to move beyond the pain that threatened to consume her.

And so, two souls adrift in the dark, each seeking solace while feeling alone in their struggle. The night was stretched out before them, a vast expanse of uncertainty and loss, but the faintest glimmer of hope began to shine within its shadows.

The crisp night air clung to Rose's skin as she stepped out of the restaurant, her breath forming delicate puffs of white in front of her. She wrapped her arms around herself, seeking warmth and solace from the cold that seemed to seep into her very bones. The bus stop loomed ahead, a beacon of refuge in the sea of uncertainty that threatened to engulf her.

"Hey, Rose," Dean called softly as he approached her, his footsteps barely audible above the quiet hum of the city. He slid onto the bench beside her, leaving enough space for her comfort but close enough to offer unspoken support. "Do you need a ride home? I'm not hurrying to get back to my place."

Rose hesitated, her heart feeling heavier than ever as she remembered the scene that had played out earlier in her apartment. "No, thanks," she finally answered, her voice wavering slightly. "I live within walking distance."

"Ah, got it." Dean nodded, sensing the sadness in her tone. He searched for something else to say, his mind racing with questions he was unsure whether to ask. "Um, did your boyfriend like the food?"

Rose was hit by a sudden and overwhelming wave of emotion, causing her to tremble with her hands tightly clasped around her purse. She struggled to hold back the bitterness that threatened her as she said, "I'm sure he found everything was how he likes it." She couldn't bear to stay seated any longer, so she pushed herself up from the bus stop and began to walk away. With each step, her pace quickened, and tears began to well up in her eyes as the weight of her emotions became too much to bear.

Dean noticed a sudden change in the demeanor of Rose walking away from him. Her face seemed to be twisted in pain, and her eyes were filled with a deep sadness that was hard to ignore. Dean quickly caught up to her without wasting any time, trying to match her stride without saying anything that could make things worse.

There was a sense of unspoken understanding as they walked together as if they knew what the other was going through. They walked silently, two wounded souls sharing a common burden, each lost in their thoughts.

As they meandered through the dimly lit streets, Rose's thoughts swirled like a whirlwind, threatening to overtake her. She could still see Dominic's face – the guilt and the shock that had danced across his features when she stumbled upon him and the other woman. The betrayal stung like a thousand tiny needles piercing her skin, leaving her raw and vulnerable in its wake.

Meanwhile, Dean racked his brain for something to say, anything to alleviate the tension between them. He knew from the depths of his heartache that sometimes, just talking about it could help. But for now, he walked by Rose's side, offering her the gift of companionship in their shared silence.

The muted glow of the streetlamps cast elongated shadows on the pavement as if reaching out to envelop Rose and Dean in their warm embrace. Side by side, they walked, their footsteps echoing through the otherwise quiet night. Despite the heaviness in his heart, Dean decided it was time he shared his troubles with her.

"Y'know," he began, a hint of self-deprecation in his voice, "I'm not in any hurry to get home tonight either. I don't have a home to go to anymore."

Rose glanced at him, her puffy eyes filled with concern, and for a fleeting moment, she forgot her pain. "Oh, Dea n... I'm so sorry. What happened?"

He sighed, running a hand through his hair. "My band and I got evicted from our apartment today. The guys decided the whole music journey was getting too complicated, so they packed up and returned to their families."

"Wow," she murmured, empathy lacing her words. "T hat's... That's a lot to deal with. Are you going back home too?" She couldn't help but feel the tiny tremor in her voice that betrayed her fear of losing a potential new friend amid her chaotic life.

Dean shook his head. His lips pressed into a thin line. "That's not an option for me." He didn't elaborate further, instead choosing to step away from her, distancing himself as he stared at the ground, trying to gather his thoughts.

Rose hesitated for a moment before following him. At this point, listening to someone else's problems seemed like a welcome distraction from her own. As she caught up with him, she gently touched his arm, urging him to share more.

"Is there anything I can do to help?" she asked softly, her voice barely above a whisper.

"Thanks, Rose, but..." Dean hesitated, a wistful smile playing at the corners of his mouth. "I think I just need to figure things out alone."

"Sometimes," she offered tentatively, "talking about it helps."

He looked at her then, really looked at her – past the tear-streaked cheeks and the anguish in her eyes – and for the first time that night, he saw a flicker of hope and determination shining through the darkness. Dean couldn't help but feel grateful to have crossed paths with someone like Rose.

"Maybe you're right," he admitted, letting out a deep breath as they continued to walk together, their shared silence slowly giving way to a newfound bond forged through adversity.

Chapter 4

Dean and Rose sat on the steps of the old, imposing building, the darkness of the night surrounding them. As they spoke, their breaths created puffs of white in the chilly air. Their conversation was easy and natural, each feeling a deep connection beyond superficial acquaintance.

Despite having only met a few hours ago, they found themselves lost in a deep, meaningful conversation that seemed to resonate with them like a familiar melody. It was as if they had known each other for years rather than just a few hours.

Dean gazed up at the star-studded sky, his eyes shining with wonder and hope. He took a deep breath and spoke softly as if sharing a secret. "I've always dreamed of being a musician," he said. "To create music that touches people's hearts speaks to their souls, and makes them feel alive." He hesitated for a moment as if unsure whether to continue before he went on.

"It's been a long and winding journey, full of highs and lows. Sometimes, I felt like giving up when I doubted myself and my talent. But I never lost sight of my dream, of the passion that drives me. And now, it feels liberating to finally share all this with someone, to speak my mind and express my true self without fear of judgment or rejection."

As Dean spoke about his innermost struggles and aspirations, Rose listened intently, her gaze warm with empathy. She could sense the weight of his thoughts and feelings that he had kept bottled up for so long, and her heart went to him. Seeing the usually cheerful Dean open up in such a vulnerable way was almost surreal for her.

Without hesitation, she leaned in, her body language conveying her willingness to listen and offer a safe space for him to share his thoughts. Her heart ached for him and his dreams; she hoped he could feel seen and heard in that moment.

As she spoke, her voice was gentle and soft. She placed her hand gently on his arm, a gesture of comfort and support. "Dean, I can't begin to imagine how difficult it must have been for you to keep all of this bottled up inside," she said sympathetically.

Her words were a testament to his trust in her, and she was genuinely grateful for his willingness to share his story with her. "Thank you for opening up and trusting me with your deepest thoughts and feelings."

As she spoke, her words profoundly impacted him. He appeared visibly relieved and more at ease, as if a heavy burden had been lifted from his shoulders. Dean's expression softened into a warm smile, and his eyes glowed with gratitude. Sensing the moment, he gently prompted her to share her story, eager to hear her perspective and learn from her experiences.

Rose took a deep breath to steady herself before recounting her harrowing tale. She explained that she had followed her boyfriend Dominic from their small town to the big city, lured by his ambition and the promise of a better life. However, things quickly worsened, and Rose was trapped in a nightmare.

Her voice shook with emotion as she spoke, and she looked away, unable to meet Dean's gaze. She explained that she had gone home to surprise Dominic with food earlier that day during her lunch break. But when she arrived, she was met with a sight that shattered her heart into a million pieces.

Dominic was with another woman, and it was clear from their intimate embrace that their relationship had been going on for some time. Rose felt a wave of shock and betrayal wash over her as she realized that the man she had followed to the big city could have been cheating on her all along. It was a devastating blow, and one that she wasn't sure she could ever recover from."

Rose, I'm so sorry," Dean whispered, his heart breaking for her.

She sighed in relief and expressed her gratitude, saying, "Thank you." The city had altered her and the person she loved dearly. She reminisced about the days when simple things brought her immense joy, but now everything seemed complex and daunting. The overwhelming nature of the city had taken over her life, and she longed for the simpler times when the little things in life were enough to make her happy.

Dean reached out and squeezed her hand, offering comfort and support. As their eyes met and held, they both knew they had found something rare and precious in each other – a connection that could be the balm for their wounded hearts.

The gentle luminescence of the streetlights bathed the steps where Dean and Rose had decided to rest, casting a warm, golden hue that enveloped them in a cocoon of coziness. The soft, ambient glow created an intimate ambiance as they delved into deep conversation, their words flowing effortlessly in the tranquil night air.

Nearby, the shadows of towering trees swayed gently, their intricate patterns dancing gracefully around the couple, amplifying the sense of seclusion and privacy they seemed to cherish in each other's presence. The once-daunting structure behind them, which had loomed with an imposing aura just hours before, now receded into the background, its formidable presence diminished to mere insignificance amidst their shared solace and connection.

Instead, their attention was focused on the small world they had created through their conversation, a world that was filled with their innermost thoughts and fears, hopes and dreams. They were lost in their little universe for the moment, utterly oblivious to the noise and chaos of the city around them.

"Dean," Rose began hesitantly, her eyes glistening with newfound courage, "there's something I haven't told anyone, not even Dominic. Before I followed him here, I had dreams of my own. I wanted to be an artist. I love to paint."

"Really?" Dean asked, surprised but curious. "What made you give up on that dream?"

"Following Dominic's dream seemed like the right thing to do at the time," she admitted, her fingers absently tracing patterns on the cold stone steps beneath her. "In hindsight, I lost myself somewhere along the way."

Dean couldn't help but feel a deep empathy for Rose as she poured out her heart to him. He knew all too well the feeling of sacrificing one's happiness for the sake of others. Looking into her eyes, he saw the pain and uncertainty that plagued her, and he knew that he had to say something to help ease her burden.

"Rose," he said softly, "it's never too late to chase your dreams. It might seem impossible now, but you are powerful, and I truly believe in you. You have so much potential, and I do not doubt you can achieve anything you want."

Dean saw a glimmer of hope in Rose's eyes as he spoke. It was clear that his words had touched her deeply, and he felt a sense of satisfaction knowing that he had been able to make a difference in her life. He knew it wouldn't be easy for her to pursue her dreams, but he also knew she could accomplish anything she wanted with encouragement and support.

"Thank you, Dean," she whispered, touched by his encouragement. "And you—how did you stay true to your passion for music despite the struggles you've faced?"

"Music has always been a part of me," he said, his voice filled with conviction. "Through every hardship, it's been my anchor, my constant. No matter how often I fall, I know I'll keep getting back up because of my love for it."

As they shared their stories of disappointment and heartbreak, they discovered solace in each other's vulnerability. It was a rare connection, borne from a mutual understanding of their struggles pursuing their dreams.

Rose looked at Dean pensively and asked, "Dean, can I ask you something? Lately, I've felt lost and uncertain about my future. Sometimes, it feels like everything is too hard, and I don't know if I can keep going. Do you ever feel that way too - like giving up is the only option?"

He looked down, his eyes filled with uncertainty. "Sometimes," he confessed in a low voice. "There are moments when I feel like giving up and throwing in the towel. But then I take a deep breath and remind myself how far I've come.

I think about the person I want to be and how much I still have to accomplish. It's that thought that keeps me motivated and moving forward." He paused momentarily before turning to me and asking, "What about you? Are you willing to give your dream another chance?"

Rose's smile was soft and kind, but a glint of newfound determination in her eyes couldn't be missed. "Yes," she said with conviction, "I think I am. And I have you to thank for that." Her words were directed at someone who now appears to be playing a new significant role in helping her reach this realization, whether through advice, support, or simply being there for her. It was clear that Rose was grateful to Dean and the impact he was starting to have on her life.

"Then we'll chase our dreams together," Dean declared, his voice full of warmth and promise.

Their hearts swelled with hope as they sat on those steps, their lives irrevocably intertwined. They had found an unexpected ally in each other, someone who understood their challenges and believed in their ability to overcome them. It was a rare and beautiful connection that would stay with them through all the twists and turns life had in store.

As the sky darkens, the moon emerges in all its glory, casting a soft and luminous light over Dean and Rose as they sit together on those worn stone steps. The city around them hums with life, offering a vibrant backdrop for their heartfelt conversation. As they delve deeper into their dreams and aspirations, fear and uncertainty give way to openness and trust, drawing them closer.

"Tell me more about your music," Rose urged, her eyes alight with curiosity. "What do you love most about playing the guitar?"

Dean's eyes sparkled with passion as he spoke, his hands instinctively mimicking the movements of strumming chords. "There's something magical about creating music, you know? I can express my emotions through the melodies and harmonies when words aren't enough."

"Music has always been my escape, a way to make sense of the world," he continued, his voice filled with conviction. "And when I'm on stage, it's as if time stands still, and there's just me and my guitar, sharing our story with the audience. That connection...it's indescribable."

Rose leaned in closer, captivated by the intensity of his words. She could almost see him on stage, pouring his heart out through every note. The thought brought a smile to her face, and she marveled at how this man, who had once been a stranger, now felt like someone she could confide in without reservation.

"Dean, your passion is truly inspiring," she said earnestly. You're meant to be a musician, and I have no doubt you'll achieve your dreams."

"Thank you, Rose," he replied, gratitude shining in his eyes. "That means a lot to me, especially coming from someone as talented and driven as you."

Dean and Rose continued to share their dreams and passions as the moon glowed above them, bathing the city in twilight. They spoke of the joy of creating art through music or painting and how it filled them with purpose and fulfillment. Having found solace in each other's company and united by their shared experiences, this newfound friendship felt like it had been years in the making.

Dean and Rose discovered the power of vulnerability and authenticity through it all, realizing they were not alone in their struggles. As the starry night sky unfolded above them, their connection deepened, offering a beacon of hope and possibility in a world that so often seemed dark and uncertain.

A gentle breeze caressed Rose's hair, a subtle reflection of the turmoil within her. Pausing, she grappled with her emotions, her hands tightly clasped in her lap. Summoning courage, she met Dean's gaze, finding solace in his unwavering attention, a sanctuary where her dreams could be shared without fear of judgment.

"Dean, I've always loved art," she began, her voice barely above a whisper, as if sharing a secret. "Ever since I was a little girl, I spent hours painting and drawing. I dreamed of becoming a successful artist someday, but life took me down a different path."

Dean watched her intently as Rose spoke, his eyes reflecting a mix of curiosity and empathy. He leaned in slightly, encouraging her to continue.

"Moving here with Dominic was supposed to be our big adventure, our chance to chase our dreams together," she said, her voice cracking ever so slightly. "But now, everything feels so uncertain. Sometimes, I doubt my abilities and wonder if I'll ever find my place in this world."

"Rose," Dean said gently, reaching out to place a comforting hand on her arm. "I understand how you feel. I've been there, too. But don't let your doubts hold you back. You're talented and have so much to offer the world." His words were sincere, and she felt a warmth spread through her at his encouragement.

"Thank you, Dean," she replied, smiling softly. "It's comforting to know I'm not alone in feeling this way."

"Of course not," he said with a reassuring grin. "We all have our struggles, but it's important to remember that we can overcome them if we stay true to ourselves and keep pushing forward."

As they sat side by side on the steps of the immense dark building, Rose felt a sense of relief wash over her. For the first time in what felt like ages, she could be vulnerable and authentic with someone who understood her struggles. In Dean's company, she found solace and understanding that made her feel less alone in this vast city.

"Dean," she said, her voice filled with newfound determination. "Let's make a promise to each other right here and now. Let's promise to never give up on our dreams, no matter how hard it gets or how many obstacles we face."

"Deal," he agreed without hesitation, his eyes shining with resolve. They shook hands to seal their pact, their fingers intertwining briefly, before leaning back against the cold stone steps, staring at the twinkling city lights.

And as the night deepened around them, Dean and Rose knew that they had found something extraordinary in one another: a connection that went beyond mere friendship, forged through shared dreams, heartache, and hope. It was a bond that would help them navigate the uncertain waters of life, reminding them that they were never truly alone.

The city lights shimmered in the night on Rose's face as she looked up at the stars, her eyes reflecting the constellations above. She felt a gentle breeze tugging at her hair, and for a moment, it seemed as if the world had stopped spinning, leaving only her and Dean sitting side by side on the lonely steps.

"Dean," Rose began hesitantly, "Can I ask you something? What's your biggest fear?"

He sighed, his breath mingling with the cool air. "Honestly, my biggest fear is never achieving my dreams. I'm afraid that one day, I'll wake up and realize I've wasted all this time chasing something never meant to be mine."

She nodded, understanding his sentiment all too well. "I feel the same way sometimes. Like, what if I'm just not good enough? What if I'm fighting hard for something just out of reach?"

"Hey," he said gently, reassuringly touching her shoulder. "We can't let our fears dictate our lives. We have to keep pushing, no matter how scary things get. We'll only know if we can achieve our dreams by trying, right?"

"Right," she agreed, smiling softly as she leaned into his comforting touch. Their shared vulnerability created an atmosphere of trust and safety, enabling them to open up to each other honestly.

As they continued to discuss their insecurities, the conversation took a lighter turn. They began teasing each other about their quirks and laughing at their embarrassing stories. Their laughter filled the night air, creating a cocoon of happiness around them.

"Okay, okay," Rose gasped through her giggles, wiping away tears from her eyes after Dean recounted a particularly hilarious tale involving a disastrous first gig. "Enough about our past embarrassments. Let's talk about something positive. What's your favorite thing about playing music?"

"Ah, that's a tough one," Dean pondered, a playful smile tugging at the corners of his mouth. "I'd have to say it's the feeling I get on stage and the connection with the people. There's something so magical about connecting with an audience like that."

"Wow, that sounds amazing," Rose responded, her eyes lighting up as she imagined him performing under the bright stage lights. "It's when I finish a painting and step back to see the whole piece come together. It's like bringing a part of my soul to life."

"See?" Dean grinned, nudging her gently with his shoulder. "We both know what we want, and we both know what brings us joy. Now all we have to do is hold onto that feeling and keep moving forward."

As their laughter and heartfelt confessions echoed into the night, they found solace in each other's presence, creating a sanctuary where they could be authentic without fear or judgment. Though they couldn't predict the future, they knew they had the strength to face whatever challenges life threw their way together.

Dean and Rose sat side by side, their shoulders touching ever so slightly. The brisk night air nipped at their cheeks, but neither seemed to notice as they continued to share their stories late into the evening.

"Thanks for listening, Rose," Dean said softly, his eyes

shimmering with vulnerability, "I don't know if I've ever been this open with anyone before."

"Me too, Dean," she admitted, brushing a stray lock of hair behind her ear. "It's like we were meant to find each other?"

Dean nodded, his gaze never leaving hers. "Yeah, it's like fate brought us together to help each other heal."

As they spoke, they both felt a growing sense of hope – a belief that maybe, just maybe, things could change for the better.

The peaceful silence of the night was abruptly shattered by a loud and startling noise - the sound of glass shattering and car alarms blaring. At first, Dean and Rose couldn't quite comprehend what was happening, but as they turned their heads in unison, their eyes were met with an alarming sight.

Across the street, three masked criminals were ruthlessly breaking into cars, their movements a frenzied blur. It was a sickening race, each criminal trying to outdo the other in a twisted game of thievery. The scene was a chilling tableau, and Dean and Rose couldn't help but feel a wave of fear and unease wash over them.

Rose turned to Dean, her face a mask of terror, her voice quivering as she spoke. "Dean, what do we do?" she asked, her eyes locked on the audacious crime spree unfolding before them.

Shattering glass and alarms blaring filled the air as they watched helplessly, unsure how to react to the chaos erupting around them. The scene was both terrifying and surreal, as if they had stumbled onto the set of a movie. But this was all too real, and they needed to figure out a plan fast before the situation spiraled out of control.

Dean's voice was a mere whisper as he spoke to her, his words a desperate plea for calm. "Stay calm," he urged, his grip on her hand tightening. His heart was a thunderous drumbeat in his chest, and a part of him yearned to intervene, but his instincts screamed at him, warning that doing so could lead to a tragic outcome.

Instead, he suggested they stay put and try to remember as much as possible about the people around them. The air was tense, and every movement felt like a threat. But they held on to each other, trying to remain still and inconspicuous, hoping they wouldn't attract unwanted attention.

Rose's breathing quickened as she glanced back and forth between the destructive criminals. Fear crept into her mind as she witnessed the chaos they were causing. The sound of shattering objects and crashing debris filled the air around her. Despite her growing anxiety, she tried to remain calm and focused on the situation at hand.

Their instincts kicked in, and they both felt an overwhelming urge to protect each other. The harrowing moment seemed to last forever, but they found comfort in their shared connection.

Despite the world spinning out of control, they felt a deep sense of trust and loyalty, making them feel like they could face anything together. As they held each other tightly, they knew they were stronger as a team, and their bond would grow.

The night had turned sinister, the chaos across the street casting a dark shadow over their newfound connection.

Dean's voice quivered slightly as he leaned towards Rose and whispered, "Please stay close to me." The tremble in his voice betrayed the fear and urgency he felt at the moment. He knew that danger was lurking nearby and didn't want to take any chances.

Rose could sense the seriousness in Dean's tone, and she nodded in agreement, silently acknowledging the need for caution. The two of them attempted to move forward, Dean leading the way, with Rose following closely behind, her eyes scanning the environment for any signs of danger.

Rose's voice shook as she turned to Dean, her eyes wide with fear. She reached out and grabbed his arm, her fingers digging into his skin as she tried to steady herself. Her heart was racing, pounding against her chest, and she felt like she couldn't breathe. "Dean, I'm scared," she admitted, her voice barely above a whisper. She looked up at him, hoping to find comfort or reassurance in his eyes.

He looked at her with a soft expression, noticing the worry in her eyes. "Me too," he admitted, his fear creeping up. He took a deep breath, trying to calm himself down before continuing. "But we've got each other, okay? We can get through this together." He spoke reassuringly, hoping to provide her some comfort and strength during this difficult time. Despite his apprehension, he put on a brave facade, determined to be there for her no matter what.

Shattering glass echoed through the quiet streets as the criminals entered the parked vehicle. They rummaged through the car, frantically searching for something valuable. Suddenly, one of them looked up and saw Dean and Rose sitting across the street, frozen in fear.

The criminal's face twisted into a menacing sneer as he yelled out to them in a threatening tone. "If it were just you two, we would've handled you both! We don't like witnesses at all!" His words hung in the air, sending shivers down Dean and Rose's spines.

Before either Dean or Rose could react, the criminals sprinted away, disappearing into the city's shadows. For a moment, they sat frozen, processing the threat that had been hurled at them. Dean's mind raced, contemplating what he could have done differently. Could he have protected Rose better? What if they had been attacked?

"Dean," Rose whispered, her voice trembling, "do you think they'll return?"

"I don't know," he admitted, his heart sinking. "But right now, let's focus on getting to safety."

"Okay," she nodded, trying to muster some courage deep within her gentle heart.

They scanned the area cautiously, ensuring the coast was clear before venturing from their spot on the steps. As they thought about moving away from the scene, Dean couldn't help but notice the stark contrast between the darkness of the night and the warmth he felt radiating from Rose's presence by his side.

"Despite everything that just happened... I'm glad I met you, Rose," Dean confessed, his voice barely audible.

"Me too, Dean," she whispered, her hand squeezing his. "We have each other to lean on now."

As chaos and uncertainty threatened to consume everything around them, Dean and Rose sought solace in each other's company. The ordeal they had just faced had been nothing short of terrifying, but their connection had only grown stronger through it all. It was as if the adversity they had faced had forged an unbreakable bond between them - one that would continue to hold them together, no matter what life threw their way.

With the fear and heartache of their recent experience behind them, they stepped forward into the unknown together, their resilience and determination a testament to their strength. They knew that whatever challenges lay ahead, they would face them head-on. Their unwavering support for each other was a guiding light through even the darkest times.

Chapter 5

As they sat side by side, the wooden door to the building let out a piercing creak, announcing the exit of a man whose face was etched with concern. The warm light that spilled out illuminated the steps that Dean and Rose were sitting on, causing their legs to brush against each other. The man scanned the area between them and asked, "Are you alright?" With apprehension, he continued, "Do you need anything?"

Dean's attention was drawn to Rose sitting next to him.

He briefly looked at her before returning to the stranger who had appeared out of nowhere. Trying to hide the nervousness in his voice, Dean asked the stranger, "Excuse me, but how long have you been standing there?" His heart raced as he wondered if the stranger had overheard the commotion outside with the car break-ins or if he was harmless.

The man standing in the back of them had a calm demeanor, with his hands casually tucked into the pockets of his worn jeans. Upon spotting the two sitting there, he approached and kindly asked, "Ah, I just came out. I saw you two sitting here and thought I'd see if everything was okay." His voice was gentle yet assertive, and his eyes showed genuine concern for their well-being.

Dean hesitated momentarily, then told this stranger about the recent events. "It was a pretty scary situation. My friend and I were sitting on these steps when we saw a group of guys breaking into cars parked across the street. We couldn't believe what we were seeing. But as soon as they noticed us, they immediately stopped what they were doing and took off running. We were left here, confused and scared, not knowing why it ended like that."

The man listened attentively, nodding sympathetically at the appropriate moments. "Sounds like quite the night," he finally remarked. I'm Dave, by the way." He introduced himself with a firm handshake. Dean noticed the callouses on his fingers and realized this man was working hard with his hands. Rose gave a small smile in response to the introduction.

"Dean," he replied, nodding towards Rose, "and this is Rose."

"Hi there, it's a pleasure to make your acquaintance," Dave said, his face displaying politeness. He went on to explain that he had been sitting in his office for quite some time, buried in work, and had decided to step outside for a moment to get some fresh air. That's when he noticed the two of you sitting here, and he thought he would come over and introduce himself.

"Your office?" Dean asked curiously, gesturing to the old brick building behind Dave.

Dave introduced himself as the church pastor with a warm and friendly smile. His eyes crinkled at the corners, conveying a sense of kindness and approachability. With his years of experience and dedication to his congregation, Dave has become a well-respected figure in the community, known for his helpfulness, compassion, and wise counsel.

Dean couldn't help but wonder about the odd turn of events as the trio exchanged pleasantries. He could feel a strange sense of comfort wash over him as if he and

Rose were meant to be there, on those steps, at that exact moment. It was a feeling he couldn't quite shake, and something deep inside him stirred.

"Thanks for checking on us, Dave," Rose said, her delicate voice laced with sincerity. "We're just trying to make sense of what happened."

"Of course," Dave replied, his gaze filled with understanding. "Sometimes life throws us curveballs, and we're left wondering why. But maybe there's a reason you two were here tonight. Who knows?"

Dean pondered over Dave's words, the possibility of a greater purpose tickling at the edge of his thoughts. He looked over at Rose, her eyes reflecting the streetlight, and was grateful for their friendship. In a world where uncertainty seemed to be the only constant, they had each other. And perhaps that was enough.

Dave gestured to the open door, his compassionate eyes sparkling under the soft glow of the streetlight. "Why don't you come inside? We have surveillance cameras around the building. Maybe they can help us figure out what happened."

"Really? That would be great," Dean replied, gratitude evident in his voice.

As they entered the church's threshold, a wave of scents greeted them, consisting of polished wood and the lingering fragrance of incense. The fragrance almost seemed to wrap around them like a warm, comforting embrace. Their footsteps echoed softly in the hollow space as they walked down the aisle, passing rows of wooden pews that had seen countless prayers and congregations.

The pews bore the marks of time, with signs of age and use evident in their worn and polished surfaces. Rose couldn't help but be amazed at the sight of the stained-glass windows adorning the walls, casting vivid hues across the floor. The colors seemed to blend and merge, creating a kaleidoscope of hues that added to the church's already serene and peaceful atmosphere.

"Is this place a church?" Rose asked in awe, her fingers brushing against the smooth surface of a nearby pew.

"Indeed, it is," Dave replied, a fond smile gracing his lips. "I'm the pastor here."

"Wow," she breathed, taking in the quiet grandeur of the space. "It's beautiful."

Dean's heart swelled with comfort and familiarity as he gazed around the sanctuary. Despite the chaos that had unfolded just outside its doors, the church seemed to radiate a deep peace within him. He could almost hear the echoes of his mother's voice singing hymns from childhood, memories he cherished now more than ever.

"Thank you," Dave said, clearly touched by Rose's

words. "This place has been a haven for many over the years. Now, let's see what we can find on those cameras."

Dave, Dean, and Rose gathered in the small office at the church's back. The room was dimly lit, and the only light source came from the large screen mounted on the wall. Dave sat in front of the screen, scrolling through the surveillance footage, searching for clues to help them identify their mysterious protectors. Dean stood to his left. His eyes fixed on the screen, and his brow furrowed in concentration.

He was determined to find any leads to help them solve the mystery. On the other hand, Rose stood to Dave's right, her hands clasped tightly together in a silent plea for answers. She couldn't shake off the feeling that something was off, and she hoped the surveillance footage could provide some insight. The three of them worked in silence. The only sounds in the room were the soft hum of the computer and the occasional sound of a mouse click.

"Wait, go back a bit," Dean instructed, pointing at the screen. "I think I saw something there."

Dave rewound the footage, and the three watched intently as the events outside replayed before their eyes and time seemed to slow down as they searched for any clue that could explain the sudden turn of events.

"See, there," Dave pointed at the screen, pausing the

video at a crucial moment. "You can tell something spooked them. But it's not what you'd expect."

"Nothing," Dean said, shaking his head in disbelief. "There's nobody else there. No one is protecting us."

Dean's mind was in chaos as he grappled with thoughts of divine intervention and unseen forces. He was utterly amazed that he and Rose had emerged unscathed from what could have been a fatal incident. Deep down, he wanted to believe that someone or something had shielded them from harm, but he couldn't shake off the feeling that life was rarely so straightforward.

He was filled with awe and wonder, but he hesitated to voice these thoughts out loud, fearing they might be dismissed as mere superstition. He knew that he had to reconcile his beliefs and doubts before fully embracing the mystery of what had just happened.

"Maybe it was just luck," he mused, forcing a half-smile. "Or maybe we did have someone watching over us."

"Whatever it was," Rose added softly, "I'm grateful."

"Sometimes, protection comes from where we least expect it," Dave said softly, his eyes meeting theirs with sincerity. "Perhaps someone was praying for you both, and those criminals saw the results of those prayers. They knew they were no match for divine intervention, so they fled."

Dean stared at him, the wheels turning as he tried to

comprehend what he'd just heard. The idea that something unseen had saved them seemed impossible, yet he
couldn't deny the evidence before his eyes.

"God is very protective of His own," Dave continued,
his voice gentle yet firm. "You both are important to Him,
and there must be something He needs you to do. That's
why you're being protected."

Rose looked back at the screen, tears welling up in her
eyes. She could feel the truth of Dave's words deep within
her soul, but it wasn't until now that she fully understood
the depth of love and care surrounding them. "What else
could explain it?" she asked quietly. "There's nothing on
the camera showing anyone there talking to us... guiding
us."

"Faith," Dean whispered, his voice cracking with emotion. "We've been so focused on what we can see that we
forgot about the power of faith."

"Exactly," Dave agreed, placing a comforting hand on
both shoulders. "Sometimes, the most powerful protection is the one we can't see."

Dean looked back at Rose, amazed by the strength and
resilience they had discovered within themselves and each
other. As they continued to watch the surveillance footage,
he couldn't help but feel awe at the divine intervention
that had kept them safe.

As they were about to leave the small office, the echoing of peace through the church, Dean and Rose knew they were not alone. They carried a newfound understanding of the power of faith and the knowledge that they were part of something much bigger than themselves.

"Thank you for all of this, Pastor Dave," Rose replied, her voice filled with gratitude as she continued to take in the beauty around her. "You can't tell how stunning it is here just by looking at the outside."

Dave nodded, his eyes twinkling with understanding. "It's true. Much like the spirit who lives inside us, sometimes people don't know what lies beneath the surface. We all have hidden depths and potential that often go unnoticed."

As Dean wanted to study the surveillance footage a little more, Rose pondered Dave's words. It was easy for her to become overwhelmed by her insecurities and fears, but the Pastor's insight reminded her that she, too, possessed inner strength and resilience.

"Pastor Dave?" Rose ventured hesitantly. "Do you think...do you think we were meant to be here today? That maybe there was a reason we ended up on those steps?"

"Rose, I believe everything happens for a reason," Dave replied thoughtfully. "Even if we don't understand it at the time, life guides us to where we need to be. Maybe this was a small reminder that you're never truly alone and that there's always someone looking out for you."

"Thank you," Rose whispered, touched by his kindness. She couldn't help but feel a sense of comfort and belonging within the church walls, something she hadn't experienced in quite some time.

Dean returned to Rose and Dave after exhausting all avenues on the surveillance footage. "Well, I think we've seen all we can for now. Thanks for your help, Pastor."

"Of course," Dave replied, clasping Dean's shoulder warmly. "Remember, you're both always welcome here."

"Please don't be strangers," Dave said, reaching for the heavy front door. "We'd love to have you visit with us again."

"Thank you, Pastor Dave," Rose replied softly but sincerely. We'll come back soon."

Dean nodded in agreement, feeling an unexpected peace within these sacred walls. As they stepped outside into the cool evening air, the tranquility of the church was replaced by the distant hum of traffic and the muted sounds of the city.

"As I said, feel free to come back anytime if you ever need a place to worship or find peace, and I will sit with you," he said sincerely.

"Take care, you two," Dave said, offering them a warm

smile before closing the door behind him.

Dean and Rose exchanged glances as they stepped back into the night, their shared experience binding them closer together. The world outside may have been unpredictable and uncertain, but within that small church, they had found a haven of hope and understanding. And with that newfound knowledge, they were ready to face whatever challenges lay ahead.

Dean couldn't help but think about the strange series of events that had brought them here as they walked side by side down the steps. It seemed fate had intervened, guiding them away from danger and towards something far more significant than they could have imagined.

"Hey," Rose said, breaking the silence between them. "Do you want to walk around the block? I'm not quite ready to head home yet."

"Sure," Dean agreed, appreciating the opportunity to spend more time together. As they turned the corner, their neighborhood's familiar sights and sounds enveloped them like a comforting blanket.

"Today has been... intense," Dean admitted, trying to put words to the whirlwind of emotions within him. "But weirdly, it's made me feel more alive than ever."

Rose looked over at him, her eyes searching his face as she tried to understand his thoughts. "I know what you mean. We've been given a second chance, and I don't want to waste it."

"Neither do I," Dean said, his heart swelling with determination and gratitude. They walked silently for a moment. Each lost in their thoughts as they processed the day's events.

As they rounded the corner once more, the golden glow of the streetlights illuminated their path, casting long shadows on the pavement. The world around them seemed to hold its breath, waiting for them to take the next step forward. As they did, Dean felt an unbreakable bond forming between them – one that would guide and protect them as they ventured into the unknown together.

"Rose," Dean began hesitantly, his voice barely above a whisper. "Back in your small town, did you attend church often?"

She looked at him, her eyes reflecting the street lights surrounding them. "Absolutely. I used to go all the time. But once I followed Dominic, I lost myself for who I was and enjoyed being."

As they walked, the rhythmic sound of their footsteps seemed to mirror the steady beat of Dean's heart, which threatened to burst with the depth of emotion he felt. He could see Rose's vulnerability and how her fingers twisted together nervously as she spoke about her past.

"Dean," she said suddenly, her voice shaky but filled with gratitude. "I need to tell you something. You know the children's story we were all raised on? About how God always leaves us breadcrumbs so we can find our way back to him?"

He nodded, waiting for her to continue, sensing the importance of what she was about to say.

"Well, I was so far gone from who I was supposed to be that I couldn't see the breadcrumbs anymore to find my way back. So, instead, God sent me to work at a restaurant where I would find a loaf of bread named Dean."

Her words hung between them, reverberating with an intensity that left Dean momentarily breathless. Was it possible that their meeting had been more than just a coincidence, that there was some greater purpose behind their connection?

"Rose, I –" he stammered, struggling to find words to express her confession's profound impact on him.

"Dean, you've helped me find my way again," she said softly, her eyes shining with unshed tears. "And I'll never be able to thank you enough for that."

As they continued their walk, the world around them seemed to fade into insignificance, leaving only the two of them and the unspoken bond that had formed between them. At that moment, Dean knew that whatever lay ahead, they would face it side by side as they embarked on a journey toward an uncertain but hopeful future.

Dean and Rose walked side by side, their shoulders occasionally brushing against each other. Both seemed lost in thought. Their eyes fixated on the ground beneath them as if they held the answers to all of life's mysteries.

"Uhm, I guess we could be the breadcrumbs we both needed," Dean finally spoke up, his voice cracking slightly. He blinked rapidly, trying to keep his emotions at bay.

Rose turned her gaze towards him, offering a small, understanding smile. "Yeah, I think so, too."

For a moment, they continued walking in silence, the only sounds being the distant hum of traffic and the rustling of leaves in the gentle breeze. Dean's mind raced with thoughts and emotions he had never experienced before. The depth of their connection and the sincerity of their bond were overwhelming yet comforting simultaneously.

Dean couldn't help but let out a soft chuckle as they passed a brightly painted fence. It felt like the entire universe had conspired to bring them together despite the obstacles and challenges they had faced.

"What's so funny?" Rose asked, her curiosity piqued.

"Nothing." Dean shook his head, his smile growing wider. "It's just... I don't know. I feel like I've found something I didn't even know I was looking for."

Rose looked at him intently, searching for an answer hidden within his words. "You mean us?"

Dean nodded, a newfound determination igniting within him. "Yeah. Us. And it's made me realize I must be there for you, Rose. No matter what happens, I want to support you just as much as I want to pursue my dreams."

"Dean..." Rose's voice wavered, touched by his unwavering devotion.

"From now on, we walk this path together," he declared, looking into her eyes with tenderness and resolve. "I've spent my life searching for something more to make me feel truly alive. And I've realized it's not just about making music – it's about sharing that journey with someone who understands me and sees the world as I do."

"Someone like me?" Rose whispered, her heart swelling with love and gratitude.

"Exactly like you," Dean replied, his voice filled with conviction.

As they continued walking, their fingers intertwined, it was as if a new chapter had begun – one filled with hope, passion, and a bond that could withstand even the fiercest storms. Together, they were strong and would face whatever challenges life had in store for them.

The magnitude of their connection weighed on them

both, yet that connection made them feel lighter than they had in years.

"Hey, Rose?" Dean ventured, his voice cracking slightly with emotion. "Yeah?" she replied, stopping momentarily to glance up at him, her eyes reflecting the moonlight.

"Promise me something," he said, swallowing hard. "Promise me we'll never let anything come between us."

Rose looked deep into his eyes, seeing the vulnerability and sincerity within. She nodded, her voice thick with emotion. "I promise, Dean. We're in this together, remember?"

A small smile tugged at Dean's mouth's corners, and he gently squeezed her hand. "Right. Together," he echoed, his heart swelling with gratitude and love.

As they resumed walking, the world seemed to fall away, leaving just the two of them and the path they forged together. Each step they took seemed to bring them closer, not only physically but emotionally as well.

"Dean, I want you to know something," Rose said softly, her words punctuated by the rhythmic sound of their footsteps. "I admire your passion for music. It's like an ember that burns brightly within you. And I think...it's time to light my ember, too."

Dean glanced at her, his eyes filled with warmth and pride. "You will, Rose. I know you will. And when you do,

I'll be beside you, cheering you on." "Thank you, Dean," she murmured, her eyes shining with unshed tears. "That means more to me than you'll ever know."

Beneath the emerging stars, Dean and Rose walked in perfect harmony, their souls intertwined and their steps synchronized. The road ahead was uncertain, filled with challenges and hardships, yet an undeniable hope radiated from their bond. And as they ventured forth into this new chapter of their lives, they did so hand in hand, knowing they were stronger together than they could ever be apart.

Chapter 6

As Rose and Dean leisurely walked down the serene street, the soft glow of the streetlights gently illuminated their path, casting a warm and inviting ambiance. The pavement beneath their feet glistened with the reflection of a thin layer of rainwater, creating a shimmering effect in the dim light.

Feeling the chill of the night air, Rose wrapped her arms around herself, seeking solace from the cold. She turned to Dean and expressed her intense hunger with a hint of longing in her voice. "Dean, I'm starving," she admitted, her rumbling stomach filling the quiet night.

Dean hesitated for a moment, glancing around to take in their surroundings. The cold night air nipped at their skin, and both felt a gnawing hunger. Dean spotted a small store up ahead as they strolled down the street. Despite the intermittent flickering of its neon sign, it appeared to be welcoming customers. With a suggestion, Dean proposed that they step inside to grab some snacks, seeking warmth and a chance to replenish their energy.

Rose beamed excitedly, her cheerful agreement evident in her beaming smile and vigorous nod. "Sounds perfect," she exclaimed, her voice brimming with enthusiasm. Her pace quickened, and she elongated her strides, eager to reach the store and immerse herself in the vast array of available products.

"Alright, let's see what we've got here," Dean said as he courteously held the door open for Rose, allowing her to enter first. As they stepped inside, they were embraced by the warm and inviting atmosphere of the store, which provided respite from the chilly air outside. A myriad of vibrant snack packages lined the shelves, enticing them in all directions."

"Look, they have those chocolate chip cookies I used to eat back in high school!" Rose exclaimed, grabbing a package off the shelf. "I remember how we'd always sneak them into the library during the study period?"

"Like you were the only one," Dean chuckled, his eyes lighting up with nostalgia. He grabbed a bag of chips from a nearby rack. "My friends had an obsession with these, too. We'd always save the crumbs at the bottom of the bag for each other."

"Those were the best part!" Rose said, laughing as she took the bag from him. They continued down the aisle, excitedly pointing out each shared favorite, their banter filling the small store with echoes of their past.

"Hey Rose, did you ever try to convince everyone that these candy bars were health food?" Dean asked, grinning as he held up a familiar wrapper.

"God, we were ridiculous," Rose laughed, shaking her head. "I can't believe anyone believed us, even for a second."

"Guess we were pretty persuasive," Dean mused, raising an eyebrow playfully.

"Or we just had very gullible friends," Rose countered, matching his teasing grin.

As they wandered through the store, their shared memories and laughter seemed to weave a cocoon around them, creating a comforting sense of familiarity. Dean felt warmth as he looked at Rose – a feeling he hadn't experienced in a long time. Her eyes sparkled with amusement, the dim lighting casting a soft glow on her cheeks.

"Isn't it funny," Rose said, her voice suddenly taking on a more somber tone, "how life can change so much, but some things stay the same?"

"Like our taste in snacks?" Dean replied, attempting to lighten the mood.

"Exactly," she smiled, a hint of sadness lingering. "Sometimes I wonder if everything would have turned out differently if we hadn't lost touch with just being who we were meant to be."

Dean hesitated, searching for words that wouldn't betray the mix of regret and longing he carried within him. Silence settled over them like a heavy blanket, punctuated only by the distant hum of the refrigerator.

"Maybe," he finally whispered, his gaze meeting hers. "But we're here now, right? That's what matters."

"Right," Rose echoed softly, her fingers brushing against his as they hunted for nostalgic snacks.

As Dean and Rose walked closer to the small grill tucked away in the corner of the store, the enticing smell of sizzling onions mixed with the mouthwatering aroma of seared beef filled the air, creating a warm and inviting atmosphere that contrasted with the cold, harsh light of the fluorescent overhead. The sight of the grill ignited a shared hunger for something heartier than their usual nostalgic snacks.

"Hey, how about we get a couple of cheeseburgers and fries?" Dean's suggestion made my mouth water, his stomach rumbling in anticipation.

"Sounds perfect," Rose replied, her eyes lighting up at the prospect of a hot meal.

As they lingered by the counter, anticipating the cook's taking their order, the warm, comforting, and inviting aroma of sizzling onions enveloped them, creating an invisible cocoon of warmth. Dean felt a solid connection to the present as if the scent anchored him to the woman beside him, which was a tangible reminder of their joyful new friendship.

"Dean, do you make your burgers at home?" Rose asked, a mischievous glint in her eyes.

"Of course," he chuckled. "The band and I would set off the fire alarm and have to eat them half-raw."

"Still one of the best meals I've ever had," she laughed, the sound warming Dean's heart.

Lost in their animated conversation, the two friends were enveloped in the comforting embrace of the quaint store's warm and inviting atmosphere. The air was tinged with fond nostalgia and cherished memories as they indulged in nostalgic reflections.

However, their idyllic interlude was rudely shattered by a sudden uproar that erupted near the front of the store. The escalating din of furious voices and heavy, hurried footsteps grew increasingly loud, prompting the two friends to exchange anxious, apprehensive glances. The serene ambiance was now veiled in an unsettling cloak of tension and unease.

Dean could sense his protective instincts awakening once more as he gazed at Rose. Tenderly, he clasped her arm and murmured, "Stay by my side." Fully aware of their potential danger, his primary concern was ensuring Rose's safety. His touch conveyed strength and tenderness, and he could feel her acknowledging his presence. At that moment, their mutual priority was to stay connected and protect each other.

"Rose's voice faltered as she cautiously spoke, her words barely audible. She hesitated with a hint of fear before asking, "Are they robbing the store?"

"Shh, just stay calm and don't attract attention," he whispered, putting a gentle hand on her shoulder to reassure her. His heart was pounding so hard that he could feel the blood pulsing in his ears. He knew they were in a dangerous situation and that every sound they made could mean the difference between life and death.

The darkness around them was thick, engulfing them

in an unsettling silence. The dim light barely illuminated the front of the store, casting long shadows that seemed to amplify Rose's fear. He longed to pull her into a reassuring embrace and promise her safety, but the grim reality held him back. All he could do was stand guard, determined to protect her and hoping against hope for their survival.

Dean couldn't shake off the internal storm raging within him. The idea of Rose being entangled in another perilous predicament filled him with a potent mix of fear and rage, coursing through his veins like a relentless tide. He grappled with the conflicting desires to shield her from harm and to avoid escalating the danger by taking action.

"Rose," he said quietly, his voice strained with worry. "No matter what happens, I need you to know that you've become very special to me."

"Dean," she replied, her eyes filling with tears. "Please don't talk like that. We'll get through this together, okay?"

"Okay," he agreed, swallowing hard as they tried their best to remain unnoticed amidst the chaos unfolding before them.

The scent of grilled onions lingered in the air as Dean led Rose more toward the back of the store, looking for a safe place to hide. The dark corners and narrow aisles felt like a maze, and he couldn't shake the sinking feeling that accompanied each step they took away from the commotion.

"Here," he whispered, pulling her behind a tall shelf lined with boxes of cereals and canned goods. Dean thought he heard the faint sound of sirens echoing in the distance, but the pounding of his own heart drowned it out. He glanced down at Rose, whose eyes were wide with fear.

"Text 911," she urged, her voice trembling slightly. "Tell them what's happening."

Dean nodded, quickly typing a message on his phone: "Robbery in progress. Hillside Market on Westwood Blvd. Two suspects, armed." When Dean hit send, he shoved the phone back into his pocket, praying that help would arrive soon.

"Check the back!" a gruff voice commanded, its tone laced with anger. "Make sure there's no one else in here!"

"Stay quiet," Dean whispered to Rose, squeezing her hand for reassurance. Their breaths came in short bursts, and he could feel her trembling beside him.

Dean's thoughts raced like wild horses, frantic from the approaching footsteps. However, a heavy sense of duty anchored him in place, compelling him to prioritize Rose's safety above all else. He knew that any hasty action on his part could jeopardize her well-being. It was a tense waiting game, where hope mingled with readiness for the fleeting opportunity that might present itself.

"Found 'em!" a voice snarled, and Dean was pulled out from behind the shelf with a sudden jerk. In the chaos, Rose's hand slipped from his grasp. A menacing figure wearing a mask seized her arm and forcefully dragged them both towards the front of the store.

"Leave her alone!" Dean shouted, struggling against the robber's grip. But the man only tightened his hold, a cruel smirk on his lips. "She's got nothin' to do with this!"

"Shut up!" the robber growled, shoving them both to their knees in front of the cashier counter.

"Open the safe, now!" the other robber demanded, waving his gun at the trembling cashier.

"I-I don't know the combination," the cashier stammered, her eyes darting down to her name tag as if it held some power over her. "I swear."

"Nice try," the robber sneered, nodding towards her name tag. Your name's right there on the tag. This is your family business. You think we're stupid?"

Dean couldn't help but notice the woman's desperation, the fear in her eyes that mirrored his own. As the robbers continued to argue with her, he turned his attention to Rose, trying to convey with a single look that they would somehow get out of this. All they had to do was hold on and wait for the right moment.

With their hearts pounding against their chests, Dean and Rose exchanged a glance, the gravity of their situation sinking in. The robbers' frustration grew palpable as they continued to argue with the cashier - desperation etched in every line on their faces.

"Look," one of the robbers said, his voice cracking with emotion as he turned his attention to Dean and Rose. "We just need money to eat, alright? That's all."

Dean held Rose's hand, reassuringly squeezing it. They remained silent, understanding that any words they spoke could add fuel to the fire.

"Fine!" the other robber snapped, his anger boiling over. He took a deep breath and let it out slowly, trying to regain control. As he did so, he caught a whiff of the grilled onions wafting in from the store's grill. His eyes widened, momentarily distracted by the aroma. "Wh-what is that smell?"

"Grilled onions," the cashier answered hesitantly, her voice shaking.

"Alright, we want whatever you're cooking, too," the robber said, pointing his gun at the cashier for emphasis. He then turned back to Dean and Rose, a hint of remorse in his eyes. "Sorry about taking your food. This wasn't supposed to involve you."

Despite the apology, Dean's heart still raced as he tried

to think of a way to diffuse the situation. Beside him, Rose trembled ever so slightly, and he wished more than anything to shield her from the terror that had befallen them.

"Please," Dean whispered, his voice barely audible, "let's just talk this through."

The robbers exchanged glances, indecision flickering across their faces. For a brief moment, hope ignited within Dean – perhaps there was still a chance to escape this nightmare unscathed.

The tension in the air was palpable as the cashier reluctantly handed over the plate of steaming cheeseburgers and fries to the robbers. Dean watched their every move, trying to glean any information to help them out of this nightmare. Rose clutched his arm tightly, her breathing shallow and shaky.

"Thanks," muttered one of the robbers before taking a bite from a cheeseburger, his eyes darting between Dean and Rose. The other robber followed suit, sinking his teeth into the juicy patty with a satisfying crunch. Their faces remained expressionless, yet Dean couldn't help but notice the subtle twitch at the corner of their mouths – a clear sign they were enjoying the food.

"Is it good?" the cashier asked hesitantly, her voice barely above a whisper.

"Shut up," the first robber growled, swallowing his mouthful of food before returning his focus to Dean and Rose. "You two, don't try anything stupid. We're just here for the money and some grub."

"Okay, we won't," Dean replied, maintaining a steady tone. His mind raced with thoughts, desperately searching for a way to protect Rose and bring an end to this ordeal. He felt her grip on his arm tighten as if she was silently pleading for him to stay calm and not provoke their captors.

"Dean," Rose whispered, her voice quivering with fear, "what are we going to do?"

"Stay calm, Rose," he thought, unable to voice his reassurances. "I'll find a way out of this somehow."

Just as the first robber brought another burger to his lips, the distant wail of sirens pierced the tense silence. A flicker of panic flashed across both robbers' faces, and they instinctively waved their guns around in a reckless manner.

"Damn it!" the second robber cursed, his voice laced with fear and frustration. "They found us!"

"Stay cool," the first robber hissed, trying to regain control of the situation. "We've still got hostages."

Dean's heart pounded in his chest, and he felt Rose tremble beside him as the gravity of their predicament became all too clear. The robbers had nothing to lose, making them more dangerous than ever.

"Please," Dean thought, a silent prayer for salvation. "Let this end without anyone getting hurt."

Dean stole a quick glance at Rose in the poorly lit store, filled with shelves of colorful candy and tempting snacks. Her eyes were wide with fear, and he longed to reach out and pull her close for comfort.

However, he knew that any sudden movement might trigger their captors. Instead, he conveyed a silent message through his gaze, hoping she would grasp his reassurance that they would overcome this ordeal together.

"Listen," the cashier said, his voice firm yet laced with understanding. This doesn't have to end badly for everyone. Just put down your guns before this gets out of control and somebody gets hurt."

The robbers hesitated, glancing nervously between each other and the approaching sirens outside. The leader's brow furrowed with uncertainty. He bit his lip as he weighed his options. His partner, a younger man with an almost boyish face, looked desperate, seemingly on the verge of tears.

"Look, we didn't want it to be like this," the younger robber said, his voice cracking. "We've just... been through a lot, you know? We've made many stupid choices, and now here we are."

Dean felt a wave of empathy wash over him as he gazed at the young man despite the apparent danger posed by the situation. Memories of his mistakes flooded his mind, leading him to contemplate the alternate paths his life could have taken.

As he observed the robbers, he couldn't help but recognize the desperation and sense of being lost hidden beneath their tough exterior. They were simply individuals trying to survive in a world they thought had seemingly abandoned them while, at some point, never letting the seeds of love grow in their hearts.

"Everybody makes bad choices," the cashier replied softly, his tone gentle but unwavering. "You still have a chance to make things right. Don't let this moment define the rest of your lives."

For a moment, all was still. The only sounds in the store were the distant sirens and the pounding of Dean's heart in his ears. Then, as if a decision had been made, the leader sighed heavily and lowered his weapon.

"Maybe you're right," he admitted, his voice barely audible. "We just... We didn't know what else to do."

"Hey, man," the younger robber said, tears streaming down his face as he looked at Dean and Rose, "we're sorry about this. You two don't deserve to be dragged into our mess."

"Let's just end this now," the cashier urged, his eyes never leaving the robbers. "You still have time to turn your lives around."

The criminals shared a prolonged, solemn gaze, silently recognizing the weight of their decision. In that instant, amid the disorder and doubt, Dean experienced a peculiar bond with these unfamiliar individuals—a mutual comprehension of human strife and the urgent quest for absolution in a world quick to pass judgment.

"Okay," the leader said finally, his voice heavy with resignation. "Let's do it."

The dimly lit store seemed to be engulfed by the passage of time, as the sound of sirens and occasional distant voices added to the overall tension. Dean glanced at the clock on the wall and was startled to see that hours had slipped since the ordeal began. Eerie shadows danced across their faces as the flickering fluorescent lights above struggled to push back the darkness.

"Attention inside the store," a voice echoed through a megaphone from outside. "This is your last warning. Come out with your hands up, or we're coming in."

Dean felt a chill run down his spine and saw Rose shivering next to him. He tried to suppress the fear gnawing at him, but his heart raced uncontrollably. Next to them, the main robber looked equally shaken, his face pale and sweat beading on his forehead.

"Look," he said, sitting down next to Dean with an air of defeat. His fingers trembled as he gripped the edge of his gun. "I never meant for any of this to happen. I just... I needed the money so bad, you know?"

"Please," Rose whispered, her voice cracking as she choked back tears. "Don't let this be how it ends."

Dean swallowed hard before speaking, his voice barely audible. "We all make mistakes, man. You still have a chance to walk away from this."

He didn't know where the words came from but felt a sudden empathy for the man. Despite everything, they were all human, each struggling with their battles. At that moment, he realized that forgiveness could be a powerful force, even when faced with dire circumstances.

"Please," he said again, locking eyes with the robber, "let us all walk away from this alive."

"Dean's right," Rose added, reaching to grip his hand tightly. You can still turn things around. You don't have to be defined by this one night."

The robber looked at them, his eyes wide with fear and uncertainty, as if weighing their words against the gravity of the situation. It seemed he might relent for a moment, but his gaze hardened, and he shook his head.

"It's too late for that now," he said, glancing towards the

windows where the police lights flashed and danced. They won't let us walk away from this after everything we've done."

"Then let us help you," Dean offered, surprising even himself with his bravery. "We'll tell them the truth – that you didn't hurt us and were going to let us go."

"Really?" the robber asked, a hint of hope creeping into his voice.

"Really," Rose confirmed, squeezing Dean's hand. "We can try, at least."

"Alright," the robber said finally, his breath hitching. "Alright, I'll... I'll do it. For all our sakes."

With that, he lowered his gun, allowing a glimmer of hope to penetrate the darkness that had enveloped them all.

The hands of the robbers trembled as they reluctantly placed their firearms onto the counter, the heavy thud sending a jolt through Dean's heart. They exchanged a final uncertain glance before slowly pivoting towards the door. With hesitant movements, they raised their hands in surrender and stepped into the blinding lights of the police cars waiting outside.

"Are you guys okay?" The cashier's voice cut through the tense silence that had enveloped the room. She wiped the sweat from her brow as she looked at Dean and Rose with genuine concern.

"Y-yeah," Dean stammered, his mind still reeling from the surreal turn of events. "We're fine, thanks to you."

"Thank you both," the cashier said, a weak smile tugging at the corners of her mouth. "I don't know what would've happened if you two hadn't spoken up."

"Neither do we," Rose replied softly, tightly gripping Dean's hand. She could feel her heartbeat thudding start to subside, but the fear lingered like an unwanted guest.

"Hey, are you guys famous or something?" the cashier asked suddenly, her eyes searching their faces for recognition.

Dean let out a small, disbelieving laugh. "No, no, we're... friends."

"Newly discovered best friends, actually," Rose added, her voice thick with emotion. She looked at Dean with gratitude and love, their connection stronger than ever after facing this life-altering ordeal.

"Must be some kind of special bond you have," the cashier mused, leaning against the counter and watching as the robbers were handcuffed outside. "Not many people would risk their lives for each other like that."

Dean glanced down at Rose, who was looking back at him with a mix of vulnerability and strength. He knew she was right – their friendship had been forged in fire and grew stronger through every trial they'd faced together.

"I guess we're just lucky to have found each other," Dean said, his heart swelling with gratitude for the woman who had been his rock and guiding light. We'll always be there for each other, no matter what."

"Always," Rose echoed, her eyes shining with unshed tears.

Dean and Rose stood together, their shoulders touching, as the blaring sirens outside were piercingly loud and painted the room with a piercing light. The flashing lights cast an eerie glow on their faces, creating a stark contrast against the darkness that surrounded them. Exhausted but undefeated, they stood united, their bond reinforced in the face of adversity.

Together, they had weathered the darkest nights, fearlessly confronting each obstacle. As they emerged victorious, their hands remained tightly clasped, a silent prayer on their lips. The experience left an indelible mark on their souls, solidifying their bond. They knew that nothing could ever shatter the strength of their new connection.

Chapter 7

Dean and Rose stood bathed in the soft glow of the moonlight on the smooth pavement, their expressions a mix of relief, gratitude, and concern as they expressed their heartfelt appreciation to the police officer who had guided them through a challenging situation. "Your help tonight means more than words can express," Dean said, his eyes reflecting a deep appreciation. "We are truly grateful for your efforts to keep us safe." Rose nodded in agreement, her voice filled with emotion as she added,

"Thank you for ensuring our safety. Your presence made all the difference, and we couldn't have navigated through this without you."

The police officer smiled, his sense of relief evident, and replied, "It's all in a day's work. I'm just glad I could be of service." The three stood there momentarily longer, basking in the night's warmth and knowing they had each other's backs.

In a soft voice, Rose shared her observation about the robbers they had encountered earlier. She noticed a fear in their eyes, making her believe they may not have acted according to their true selves. While she didn't condone their behavior, Rose thought that perhaps their actions resulted from the fear they felt at that moment.

The police officer gave Dean and Rose a solemn nod, his eyes reflecting a sense of gratitude for their empathy towards his work. "It's not always black and white out here," he said, his voice laced with a sense of weariness that hinted at the complexities of his job.

He paused momentarily, gathering his thoughts before adding, "Take care of yourselves and each other." His words carried a weight that spoke of the harsh realities of the world he worked in, leaving Dean and Rose both grateful for his service and humbled by the challenges he faced.

As the reassuring sound of the police car faded into the distance, Dean and Rose walked away, hand in hand, seeking solace in the quiet night. Their breaths mingled with the cool air, hearts racing from the harrowing encounter.

"Are you okay?" Dean asked, the worry on his face now directed at the woman beside him.

Rose nodded, but her thoughts betrayed her. She was no stranger to vulnerability, but tonight's events had shaken her. As if sensing her turmoil, Dean led her toward a nearby park, where a wooden bench under a canopy of trees offered the perfect respite.

They sat down, their shoulders brushing against each other. The warmth of their connection provided a sense of security amidst the chaos. Rose closed her eyes, taking in the scent of the earth and the damp grass, letting the serenity of nature wash over her.

"Dean..." she murmured, her voice barely discernible over the gentle rustling of the leaves. "What happened there got me thinking about all the wrong turns we can take in life and how easy it is to lose sight of who we are."

"Sometimes, all it takes is one person to help us find our way again," he replied, gently squeezing her. "I'm here for you, Rose."

"Thank you, Dean," she breathed, her body relaxing into his embrace as they sat silently. Their hearts found solace in the quiet communion of two souls seeking comfort in one another.

Under the veil of night, the park seemed to take on a life of its own. The whispering wind swirled around them like a gentle caress, and the distant chirping of crickets filled the silence as Dean and Rose sat side by side on the bench.

"Dean," Rose murmured, her voice trembling slightly, "I can't help but feel sorry for those guys. Not for what they did to us – because it was a crime, and it terrified me. I feel sorry for them because they were so lost, so far from the path they should have been on."

Dean nodded slowly, his gaze fixed on the patterns of light and shadow playing across the grass. "It's like they couldn't see their way back, like they were led astray and didn't know how to find their purpose again."

"Exactly," Rose whispered, her eyes shimmering with unshed tears. "And it scares me to think we could make a wrong turn in life just as easily."

"Rose," Dean said softly, turning to face her, his eyes filled with sincerity, "that's why I'm so grateful for you. You're like the breadcrumbs God sent to guide me back to my true self. Who knows where I would be without you?"

A small smile tugged at the corners of her lips, but the sadness remained in her eyes. "I'm the one who should be grateful, Dean. You've helped me reset my life and find hope when all I could see was darkness."

They found solace in each other's understanding and compassion as their eyes locked. They discovered strength in their shared experiences and a renewed sense of purpose.

"Promise me something, Rose," Dean implored, his voice barely above a whisper. "Promise me that we'll always be there for each other, to help steer one another back on course when we lose our way."

"Dean," Rose replied, her voice full of warmth and conviction, "I promise."

With their hearts lighter and their souls intertwined, they sat together in the stillness of the night, bound by a connection forged in the crucible of life's trials.

A soft, soothing breeze danced through the trees' leaves while nestled on the worn park bench, painting the ground with moving shadows in the moonlight. Rose's hands trembled with nervousness as she reached into her pocket, pulling out a small bottle of pills. Dean's eyes widened with concern as he quickly glanced at the label, his heart pounding with worry about what he might discover.

"Rose, what are those?" His voice held a note of urgency as he waited for her answer.

Her gaze was fixed on the pills. Large teardrops were welling up in her eyes, but she made a valiant effort to keep them from spilling over. "I took these pills from my medicine cabinet tonight," she said, her voice barely above a whisper, "when I caught Dominic with that other woman." Her words trailed off, and she swallowed hard before continuing.

"I was so hurt, so devastated. I felt like my whole world had crumbled around me, and I didn't know what to do or where to turn. The pain was just too much to bear, and I just wanted it all to go away quickly, fast, and in a hurry." She paused, her voice trembling. "The level of loss I felt was indescribable. I doubt I'll ever be able to explain it fully."

Dean's chest tightened as he imagined what could have been. He gently took the bottle from her hand and wrapped his fingers around hers. Relief washed over him like an incredible wave, and he was so grateful she hadn't gone through with it. "I'm just so thankful you didn't do anything drastic, Rose. You have no idea how much you mean to me."

"Really?" Her voice was soft and vulnerable, but there was genuine curiosity in her eyes.

"Absolutely," Dean affirmed, his gaze never leaving hers. "You've been such a beacon of light and hope for me, especially on a night like this. Everything could have gone wrong if I didn't have the hope you bring to me. You keep me grounded, remind me of who I am and what's truly important."

The corners of her mouth quirked upwards in a tentative smile, and she squeezed his hand. "I guess we both needed each other, huh?"

"More than you know," Dean agreed, his smile mirroring hers. He realized then that their connection was more profound than mere friendship and marveled at how life had unexpectedly brought them together.

"Dean," Rose began hesitantly, her gaze still fixed on the pills in his hand. "I think... I think it was the devil at work when I found Dominic with that other woman. He wanted me to feel so lost and broken that I'd give up. But he didn't count on you being there for me." She looked up at him, her eyes shimmering with unshed tears. "You're that loaf of breadcrumbs, leading me back to who I'm supposed to be. Maybe I needed to get off track momentarily to find my way to you."

Her words struck a chord within Dean's heart, resonating with his experiences and hopelessness. For a moment, he was at a loss for words, overwhelmed by the intensity of their connection. Finally, he managed a shaky smile, his grip on her hand tightening. "Rose, we're both finding our way through this crazy world, but we can do it together. We're stronger together than apart."

A sense of peace settled over them, and Rose allowed

herself to lean into Dean for the first time, her head resting on his shoulder. It felt like a natural progression of their relationship, a physical manifestation of the emotional bond that had grown between them. Dean instinctively wrapped an arm around her, pulling her closer as they both reveled in the newfound comfort and security they found in each other.

As they sat on the bench, staring at the peaceful night, Dean couldn't help but reflect on the journey that had led them to this point. The trials and tribulations they had faced seemed to pale compared to the strength they found in one another. And as Rose's breathing slowed, her body relaxing against him, he knew they had both come home in a way neither had ever experienced.

"Rose," Dean whispered, his voice barely audible above the sound of the wind. "No matter what we face, I'll always be here for you. We're in this together."

"Thank you, Dean," she murmured, her words muffled by the warmth of his shoulder. "I couldn't ask for a better friend... or a better loaf of bread."

They shared a quiet laugh, and Dean felt a warmth spread through his chest, a happiness he hadn't known in a long time. As they sat there, embraced by the night, their hearts beat in unison, a testament to the power of love and friendship.

"Rose," Dean began, his voice low and earnest. "I've never felt at home like this before, you know? I've been drifting for so long, but with you here... it's like everything has finally fallen into place."

"Dean," she replied, her voice barely more than a whisper. "My heart has never felt safer than it does now. I've found the missing piece, which I didn't even realize was gone."

As Dean listened to her words, he realized how much truth there was in what she said. He had always been searching for something, trying to find his way through life, but it wasn't until Rose entered his world that he felt truly grounded. Their friendship had blossomed into something more profound and meaningful, a connection that transcended the mundane realities of everyday life.

"Maybe we were meant to find each other, Rose," he mused out loud, his heart swelling with emotion. "Maybe all those hardships we faced led us here—to this moment."

"Perhaps they did," she agreed, her eyes shining with unshed tears. "I believe that everything happens for a reason, Dean. And I think we were meant to be in each other's lives."

As they spoke, their hands found one another, fingers intertwining as if they had always belonged together. Dean could feel the steady pulse of Rose's heartbeat through their entwined fingers, a rhythm that seemed to echo his own.

They sat in companionable silence, the weight of their words settling around them like a comforting embrace. In that moment, as the world continued to spin on its axis, they found solace and safety in one another's presence—an unshakable bond that would stand the test of time.

As the moon continued its journey across the sky, Dean Winchester and Rose Evans knew they had found something rare and precious—a sense of home and security that only comes from truly connecting with another soul. In each other's presence, they found a sanctuary, a refuge from the chaos of the world, a beacon of hope that whispered, 'You are not alone.'

The night unveiled a seemingly endless canvas of velvety darkness adorned with an innumerable array of shimmering stars. Dean found solace in the gentle rhythm of Rose's breathing as she nestled close to him, their heartbeats gradually returning to a steady pace following the harrowing experience they had shared. The fading rush of adrenaline gave way to a profound sense of wonder at their strength in facing their trials together.

"Dean," Rose whispered, her voice barely audible over the gentle rustle of leaves in the breeze. "I still can't believe what happened back there...how we managed to get through it."

'Me neither,' he admitted, tightening his arm around her. 'But we did. We came out stronger on the other side. Our journey, though arduous, has only fortified our spirits, proving that together, we can weather any storm.'

Rose reached for his hand, her fingers weaving through his in a delicate embrace to emphasize their newfound connection. It was a simple gesture, yet it held a world of meaning - a silent affirmation of their unbreakable bond.

"Look at the stars," she murmured, lifting her free hand to trace the constellations above. "They seem so far away, but they're always there, shining their light on us."

Dean followed her gaze, marveling at the celestial tapestry that seemed to stretch forever. He thought back on the paths that had brought them both to this moment, the challenges and heartaches they had endured. It was as if each star represented a trial they had overcome, illuminating their way forward. In their distant brilliance, the stars whispered of a grand design, a plan that had brought them together, a plan yet to unfold.

"Sometimes I wonder if maybe the universe has a plan for us," Rose continued, her soft voice laced with wonder. "Maybe all the hardships we've faced were meant to bring us here—to help us find each other."

"Maybe it does," Dean agreed, his heart swelling with

gratitude for the woman beside him. "And I can't think of anyone I'd rather walk this journey with."

Their eyes met, and in that fleeting instant, they found solace in each other's gaze. It was a connection forged in the crucible of adversity, a testament to their shared resilience and unwavering devotion.

As they gazed up at the star-filled sky, the weight of their fears seemed to lift, replaced by the knowledge that they would never walk alone, no matter where their paths might lead.

The chilly night air seemed to lose its bite. And with each passing moment, as the stars above continued their eternal dance, Dean and Rose felt the stirrings of something more profound taking root within their souls.

Chapter 8

I t was one of those evenings when the world seemed to hold its breath, waiting for something extraordinary to happen. Dean and Rose walked side by side, their footsteps echoing softly on the pavement, each lost in their thoughts.

"Can you hear that?" Rose asked, her voice barely a whisper. She was adding an eerie tension to the already dark and foreboding atmosphere.

Dean strained his ears, trying to pick up the source of

the distant sound that had caught his attention. After a moment, he caught the faint but unmistakable sound of furious voices carried on the wind. Glancing at Rose, he noticed the concern on her face, her brow furrowed with worry. "Yeah," he replied, his unease settling like a heavy-weight in his chest. "It sounds like people arguing."

"Should we... I don't know. Can you do something?" Rose's empathetic nature compelled her to want to help, but she hesitated, unsure of what they could do.

"Let's get closer, but not too close," Dean suggested, remembering how their previous attempt to intervene in a heated situation had ended in disaster. "We'll stay at a safe distance this time."

As they strolled down the narrow, dimly lit street, the heated argument between some people seemed to inten-sify, each word becoming sharper and more precise. The tension in the air was so thick that it felt almost tangible, weighing heavily on Dean and making it challenging for him to maintain his usual lightheartedness. He couldn't help but notice the subtle quiver in Rose's hand as it brushed against his, a clear indication of her escalating anxiety.

"Are we close enough yet?" Rose whispered, her eyes darting nervously around the darkening street.

"Almost," Dean replied, focusing on the source of the

commotion. They took a few more cautious steps, careful not to draw attention to themselves, and finally came to a halt behind a tall hedge.

"Stay here," Dean instructed, trying to reassure her with a smile. "I'll make sure everything's okay."

"Be careful," Rose implored, her voice strained with worry.

"Always am," Dean said, winking at her before returning to the scene unfolding before them.

From their vantage point, they could see a couple standing on the front lawn of a house, their faces contorted in anger as they hurled accusations at one another. The man's voice trembled with desperation as he implored his wife to understand and forgive him, while the woman's eyes blazed with a mixture of fury and deep hurt, rendering her inconsolable. The tension in the air was palpable as accusations flew between them, creating a scene fraught with raw emotion.

"Can't they just talk it out?" Rose wondered aloud, her heart aching for the couple. "Why does everything have to be so... intense?"

"Sometimes, people need to let it all out," Dean murmured, torn between his desire to comfort Rose and his instinct to protect her from harm. "The important thing is that we're here if they need help."

Dean couldn't help but think about the fragile balance of love and trust as they continued to watch from a safe distance. How easily it could shatter, leaving only fragments of what once was. He hoped that he and Rose would never find themselves in such a situation, their friendship and bond too strong to be broken by anything life threw their way.

The house's front door swung open violently, echoing through the quiet street. The wife reemerged, her face flushed and tear-streaked, clutching another armful of clothes. She hurled them onto the lawn, an eruption of fabric and frustration.

"See if you can find somewhere else to sleep tonight!" she screamed at her husband, who stood helplessly on the porch, wringing his hands.

Dean cringed as he watched the scene unfold, feeling the raw emotion emanating from the couple like heat from a fire. Beside him, Rose's grip on his hand tightened, her empathetic heart aching for the pain they were witnessing.

"Can't we do something?" she whispered, looking up at Dean with eyes that seemed to hold all the sorrow in the world. He knew she wanted to help, but he also knew that sometimes, people needed to fight their battles.

"Let's just watch for now," he replied softly, hoping the couple could find a resolution before things escalated.

As if summoned by the chaos, more neighbors emerged from their homes. Some attempted to shield their children's eyes from the unsettling scene, while others watched unabashedly. A few exchanged knowing glances, hinting they had witnessed similar events before and knew what would happen next.

"Whose side are you on?" one neighbor asked another, clearly drawn into the drama unfolding before them.

"Right now, I'm just worried about them both," the other neighbor replied, a somber expression on his face.

Dean couldn't shake the feeling that they were all intruding on an intensely private moment, like peering through a window into someone else's pain. But at the same time, he couldn't look away. The intensity of the argument, the raw emotions on display, held him captive.

"Maybe we should go," Rose suggested, her voice wavering slightly. "This feels... wrong."

"Let's give it another minute," Dean said quietly, his heart heavy with what they witnessed. As much as he wanted to protect Rose from the horror of the world, he knew that sometimes, there was no hiding from it.

"Okay," Rose agreed reluctantly, her fingers still entwined with his. Together, they watched as the scene unfolded, a haunting reminder of how fragile love could be.

The wife's voice cracked like a whip, slicing through the

night air. "You never appreciate me!" she screamed, her face contorted with pain and anger.

Dean winced at the raw emotion in her voice, feeling as if he were intruding on their private moment. He glanced at Rose, whose eyes brimmed with tears, reflecting the empathy that was her trademark.

"Baby, I do appreciate you," the husband countered defensively, his hands outstretched in a futile attempt to bridge the chasm between them. "I do."

"Then tell me how!" the wife demanded, her eyes wide and desperate. "Tell me all the ways you appreciate me!"

"Right here? Now?" the husband asked, his face flushing with embarrassment as he became acutely aware of their growing audience.

"Tell me!" the wife insisted, her voice breaking.

Rose squeezed Dean's hand, seeking comfort in his familiar touch as they bore witness to the couple's unraveling. Dean couldn't help but think about their new relationship and how easily such deep-rooted issues could surface and threaten even the strongest bond.

"Okay," the husband acquiesced, swallowing hard. "I appreciate how you take care of our home, make every meal special, and always have a kind word for everyone you meet."

The wife's posture softened slightly, but her expression

remained resolute. "Go on," she urged, her voice now low and dangerous.

"Uh, I... I appreciate how you support me in my job and how patient you are with me when I'm stressed or tired," the husband continued, searching for the right words. "And... and how you laugh at my stupid jokes even when they're not funny."

Dean reflected on his feelings for Rose as the husband spoke and how her presence had become both a balm and a beacon in his life. He felt a sudden surge of gratitude for her and an overwhelming desire to protect her from the pain that surrounded them.

"Is that it?" the wife asked, her voice cold and unforgiving.

"Please," the husband pleaded, "let's go inside and talk about this."

"No," the wife snapped, her eyes blazing with fury. "I want to hear it all. Right here. Right now."

The couple stood locked in a standoff, the tension between them palpable and heavy. Dean could only watch helplessly as their love slowly crumbled before his eyes, reminding him how fragile even the strongest bonds could be if left untended.

Once flushed with anger, the wife's face suddenly stilled, almost unnerving. Her dark and searching eyes bore into her husband's soul as she asked him pointedly, "Am I pretty?"

Glancing around at the gathering crowd of neighbors, the husband shifted uncomfortably. "Why are we doing this out here? Can't we go inside and talk about this?"

"Answer the question," she insisted, her voice barely above a whisper but laced with an intensity that sent shivers down Dean's spine. He could see her vulnerability beneath the bravado and recognized it for what it was—a desperate plea for reassurance and love.

Before the husband could respond and without warning, a radiant trail of light suddenly cut through the darkness, seizing the attention of everyone in the vicinity. A collective gasp filled the air as the unexpected splendor of the shooting star entranced the crowd.

Its luminous tail blazed a mesmerizing path through the night, leaving behind a shimmering wake of stardust. The moment was so captivating that time seemed to stand still as the mesmerized onlookers gazed in awe at this celestial display, an undeniable reminder of the breathtaking beauty inherent in the cosmos.

"Make a wish," Rose whispered beside him, her voice tinged with awe and hope—starkly contrasting the turmoil unfolding before them.

Tears glistened in her eyes. The wife seemed momentarily captivated by the celestial event. She closed her eyes briefly, and when they opened again, they held a fierce determination. "I need to know right now," she said, her voice shaking with emotion. "I just made a wish, and you had better start talking."

As Dean watched the scene unfold, his heart ached for the couple who were so clearly struggling to find their way back to one another. The raw honesty of their pain resonated within him, and he reflected on his relationship with Rose. Amid the chaos, could they, too, find the strength to hold onto each other?

"Of course you're pretty," the husband stammered, his expression a mixture of confusion and desperation. "You've always been beautiful to me."

"Then why don't you tell me?" the wife demanded, her voice breaking.

"Tell you?" he asked, momentarily taken aback.

"Tell me I'm pretty. Tell me you love me. Or maybe... maybe you don't anymore." The vulnerability in her eyes was almost too much for Dean to bear, and he felt a surge of protectiveness toward this woman he barely knew.

"Of course I do," the husband insisted, reaching out to touch his wife's arm. "I love you, and I think you're beautiful. But please, let's go inside and talk about this."

The simple admission seemed to carry the weight of the

world with it, and as Dean watched the couple locked in their struggle, he couldn't help but wonder what would become of their love story—and of his own.

"Please," the wife whispered, her voice barely audible, "just tell me I'm pretty."

"Fine," the husband sighed, finally relenting. "You're pretty. You're the most beautiful woman I've ever known."

For a moment, it seemed as though the storm had passed. As they stood beneath the stars, holding both their wishes and fears, Dean couldn't help but hope that somehow, love would find a way to heal them all.

The soft, amber light of the street lamps enveloped the scene, creating a serene atmosphere that contrasted sharply with the intense emotions playing out before Dean and Rose. The flickering light threw elongated shadows that seemed to waltz across the pavement, adding an eerie yet captivating element to the unfolding drama.

As Dean and Rose locked eyes, their unspoken connection pulled them closer to the emotional storm unraveling before them. Each tentative step seemed to echo the uncertainty in their hearts, yet the magnetic pull of the unfiltered human experience ahead was impossible to resist.

"Is she going to keep pushing him like this?" Rose whispered, her voice wavering with empathy. She bit her lip, her eyes filling with unshed tears as she identified all too well with the woman's desperate need for validation.

"I don't know," Dean admitted, his heart aching for the husband and wife locked in this painful dance. "Maybe they just need to hear it from each other."

As if responding to their thoughts, the wife closed the distance between her and her husband, her eyes pleading for the reassurance she craved. "Tell me again," she demanded, her voice cracking under the weight of her vulnerability.

"Please," the husband implored, his cheeks flushing with embarrassment as he glanced at the gathering crowd. "Let's go inside and talk about this privately."

Dean could see the sincerity in the man's eyes, the desire to mend the rift that had opened up between them. But he also understood the wife's longing for public affirmation – an acknowledgment that she was worthy of love, not just behind closed doors but in every aspect of their lives.

"Come on," Dean murmured to Rose, gently tugging her arm as they edged closer to the couple. He could feel the tension in the air, thick and palpable, as if it were a living, breathing entity that threatened to swallow them whole.

"Isn't this enough?" the wife asked, her voice barely audible amidst the emotions that swirled around them.

"Can't you just tell me I'm pretty right here?"

"Of course," the husband conceded, his voice heavy with resignation. "You're beautiful. You've always been beautiful to me."

The words hung like a promise, and Dean felt something shift inside him. It was as if they were witnessing the first tentative steps toward healing—not just for this couple but for their unspoken fears and insecurities.

"Maybe that's all any of us need," Rose whispered, her hand resting lightly on Dean's arm, a silent acknowledgment of the connection that had drawn them together in friendship and beyond. "Someone to remind us of our worth."

The soft glow of the streetlights enveloped the couple as they stood in the middle of their front lawn, their faces illuminated with mixed emotions. Dean observed the wife's eyes, which conveyed a potent blend of hurt and unwavering determination as they locked onto her husband's.

"We will talk about it right now," she insisted, strained but resolute. "Because I hear you tell one of our neighbors that another neighbor was pretty, you will tell me I'm pretty in front of the whole world, too."

Dean glanced at Rose, whose empathetic gaze mirrored his concern. This conversation had been brewing for some time, and each word spoken like a tightly coiled spring was finally released. He couldn't help but feel sympathy for the husband, caught in the crosshairs of a conversation he wished to have in their home's sanctuary.

"Look," the husband said, his voice wavering as he sought to appease his wife, "I understand you're upset, and I'm sorry. But let's take this inside, please." His pleading eyes scanned their surroundings, taking in the crowd gathered – neighbors watching from porches and sidewalks, drawn by the siren call of human drama.

Dean felt a knot growing in his stomach, his insecurities and fears bubbling to the surface. He knew how it felt to be judged, to have his worth questioned. As he stood there, hand in hand with Rose, he realized that all they truly wanted was validation, reassurance that they mattered to someone.

As the husband tried to guide his wife back toward their house, she shook her head, stubbornly planting her feet on the ground. "No," she said firmly, looking him straight in the eye. "You need to say it here, in front of everyone. I need to know that you see me and think I'm just as beautiful as the other women in this neighborhood."

"Alright," the husband sighed, his shoulders slumping in defeat. He raised his voice so that everyone could hear him. "You're gorgeous. You always have been, and you always will be."

A hushed silence fell over the onlookers, the moment's weight settling heavily upon them. Dean felt Rose's grip tighten on his hand, a silent testament to their shared understanding of the importance of vulnerability and honesty. They both knew that no matter where life took them, they would strive to be each other's unwavering source of support and affirmation. And perhaps, ultimately, that made their friendship so special – the willingness to lay bare their hearts, even when it felt like the whole world was watching.

The wife's eyes blazed with defiance, a fiery determination that refused to be extinguished by the humiliation of their public argument. With deliberate slowness, she unbuttoned her blouse, her knuckles turning white from the intensity of her grip. "Do you think I'm pretty now?" she asked, her voice trembling ever so slightly.

Dean and Rose exchanged glances, the vulnerability in the wife's actions stirring a deep empathy. They moved closer, drawn to the unfolding drama like moths to a flame. The tension in the air was palpable as they edged toward the couple, their hearts pounding in sync with each step they took.

"Dean and Rose were surprised as a gruff voice shattered the eerie silence around them. They turned to see Tim, an unkempt man, emerging from a large cardboard box on the sidewalk, a mischievous smile tugging at his lips. "Can you two get out of my way?" he asked, his tattered clothes dusted with dirt. "This is my evening entertainment," he explained playfully. "I don't barge into your home and block your TV, so don't block mine."

"Sorry, Sir," Dean apologized softly, his cheeks flushing with embarrassment as he recognized the homeless man standing nearby. He and Rose exchanged glances before carefully moving to the side, giving Tim an unobstructed view of the quarreling couple.

"Thanks," Tim murmured, feeling contentment as he settled back against the rough, uneven wall of his card-board makeshift abode. A faint twinkle of amusement danced in his eyes as he observed the scene unfolding be-fore him, taking in every detail with a quiet sense of satis-faction.

Both intrigued and disturbed by the rawness of the mo-ment, Dean couldn't help but wonder what it would take to bring someone to such a desperate state. What kind of pain must they hide, buried beneath bravado and false smiles?

Rose's hand found its way into his once more, her fin-gers curling around his in a gesture of silent comfort. They stood side by side, their hearts heavy with the weight of the unspoken words and buried emotions that seemed to reverberate through the air like a collective heartbeat.

"Is this what love is?" Rose whispered, her breath warm against Dean's ear. "Baring our souls to each other, even when it hurts?"

"Maybe," he replied softly, unable to tear his gaze away from the couple. "Or maybe love is learning to see the beauty hidden beneath the scars – and having the courage to show our own."

Together, they watched as the wife's hands fell to her sides, her blouse hanging open to reveal the vulnerability she could no longer conceal.

In that brief, almost imperceptible moment, it felt like time had paused, and the entire world held its breath. In that suspended instance, the delicate interplay of love and pain unfolded like an intricate dance, casting its profound and captivating spell upon the stage of life.

Chapter 9

As the darkness of the mood descended, it left behind the lingering repercussions of this intense argument between the husband and wife, slowly dissipating, giving way to a heavy, stifling silence. The previously inquisitive neighbors gradually withdrew to the sanctuary of their homes, leaving Dean and Rose alone, illuminated by the soft, golden glow emanating from the streetlight above.

"Hi," Tim began again, his warm voice cutting through

the quiet evening as he correctly introduced himself. "I'm Tim." His eyes, full of wisdom and understanding, met Dean's and then Rose's, creating a brief but meaningful connection between them.

"Hey, I'm Dean, and this is Rose," Dean replied, his smile returning to his face in the presence of this newfound friend.

Tim nodded, looking around at the now-empty street. "Don't worry about them," he said with a comforting tone, observing the lingering concern on Dean and Rose's faces. "The couple across the street will be fine. It happens all the time."

He could feel their gazes still fixed on him, curiosity mingling with empathy. A small smile tugged at the corners of Tim's lips as he tried to lighten the mood. "I would invite you both inside," he joked, gesturing toward his humble cardboard abode, "but I'm in the middle of redecorating or relocating, whichever sounds good to you."

Dean chuckled, grateful for Tim's ability to find humor despite his circumstances. Rose, however, couldn't quite shake her sadness. Her heart ached for Tim, who was not only homeless but also able to put others at ease while he struggled.

"Thank you for saying that," she murmured, her voice barely audible. "We appreciate your kindness."

"Of course," Tim replied, his eyes twinkling with sincerity. "You two seem like good people. It's always nice to meet kindred spirits in this world."

As they stood there in conversation, their connection deepened. It was more than just a shared experience on a quiet street; it was a moment of understanding that transcended their lives. Dean grew grateful for Tim's presence, while Rose found solace in the man's unyielding resilience.

"Listen," Tim said earnestly, his gaze flitting between them, "always remember to be kind to yourselves and each other. You never know what someone is going through, so try to make their day a little brighter."

"Thank you, Tim," Rose whispered, her eyes glistening with unshed tears. "We'll do our best."

"Absolutely," Dean agreed, his voice thick with emotion.

As they stood there on that quiet street corner, their hearts a little heavier yet filled with hope, they knew that this encounter would be one they would carry with them for the rest of their lives.

The sky above was an inky black canvas dotted with stars, casting a serene glow upon the city street. Dean and Rose stood there, still processing the night's events, when Tim motioned toward his makeshift home with a grin.

"Hey, why don't you two take a seat? You look like you

could use a break," he suggested warmly. He reached inside his cardboard box and pulled out three folding chairs, setting them up on the sidewalk. The gesture was simple, yet it held a sense of dignity that seemed to defy his circumstances.

"Thank you," Dean said as he and Rose settled into the proffered seats, their eyes lingering on him with curiosity and concern.

Tim sat beside them, the air growing heavier with unspoken questions. It wasn't long before he sighed and broke the silence. "How long have you been living like this, Tim?" he asked himself aloud, mimicking their previous unspoken thoughts.

Dean frowned, taken aback by the sudden change in conversation. "Sir, we didn't say that to you."

"Maybe or not," Tim acknowledged with a wry smile, "but I know you were thinking it, so I cut through all the ice." His eyes met theirs, reflecting both vulnerability and strength. "I'm an open book. Ask me anything."

Dean glanced at Rose, who returned his gaze with equal uncertainty. It was clear that Tim was willing to share his story, but they didn't want to pry or make him uncomfortable. However, it was also evident that Tim wanted them to understand, to see him for who he was - a man who had faced adversity and come out stronger for it.

"Alright," Rose started hesitantly, her voice gentle but firm. "Tell us about your life before... this."

Tim got up from the folding chair and walked around with his hands in his pockets. He tried to conceal his face, shielding himself from their gaze if he became emotional. Dean and Rose exchanged glances as he walked, feeling the moment's weight.

He smiled sadly at her question, nodding as if he had been expecting it. "That's a good question, Rose," he said, his voice soft and tinged with resignation. "If I had to sum it up, it's due to my choices."

Dean leaned forward, concern etched across his face. "Do you regret your choices?" he asked gently.

"Of course, I have regrets," Tim admitted, pausing to look at the night sky. "There were times when I could've made better decisions and chosen a different path. But dwelling on those regrets won't change anything. I can only move forward and try to make amends for my past actions."

As he spoke, Rose couldn't help but feel a pang of empathy for the man standing before them. Here was someone who had faced unimaginable challenges yet still found the strength to carry on. She admired his resilience and wondered how he managed to maintain such a positive outlook on life despite his circumstances.

"Sometimes we make mistakes," she said softly, her eyes meeting his. "But that doesn't mean we can't learn from them and grow. You've shown us the importance of kindness and understanding, even when life seems unfair."

Dean marveled at the resilience of the human spirit as they listened to Tim. Despite the hardships that life had thrown at him, Tim remained standing, a testament to his strength and determination.

"Sometimes," Tim mused, "it's not about where we end up but how we choose to face the journey. We all have our struggles, our battles to fight. But it's how we confront them that defines who we are."

His words echoed within Dean's mind, striking a chord deep within his heart. They resonated with his hidden insecurities and fears as a timely reminder that life's trials were meant to be faced head-on.

At that moment, they were no longer strangers - they were friends, bound together by a shared understanding of life's complexities.

There was a warm, golden glow on Tim's face as he paced back and forth, his footsteps echoing softly in the quiet night. His eyes seemed distant, lost in the labyrinth of his memories, as if searching for something just out of reach.

Dean and Rose exchanged worried glances, their concern evident in the furrow of their brows and the tight set of their lips, before turning their attention back to the homeless man who seemed to be carrying the weight of the world on his shoulders.

"Okay," Tim sighed, finally stopping in front of them. "I did some bad things when I was younger, and it landed me in prison for a while."

Dean leaned forward, curiosity burning in his eyes. "What did you do?"

Tim's lips twitched into a mischievous smile, and suddenly, he spun around, his eyes wide and intense. "Murder," he whispered.

Dean and Rose gasped, recoiling in shock. Tim let out a hearty laugh, waving his hand dismissively. "Nah, I'm just messing with you. It wasn't murder."

Relief washed over the couple as they shared a nervous chuckle. Tim sat back down, his laughter fading into a somber expression. "When I was younger, I lost my way. I had just returned from living with my uncle for some years, and once I got home, I didn't know what to do next, so I hung out with people who thought having things we didn't buy was fun." He paused, staring at the ground. So we took stuff from the homes of those with many things."

Rose's empathetic nature shone through as she listened intently, her heart aching for Tim. She could see the pain etched on his face, the weight of his actions heavy on his shoulders.

Dean couldn't help but wonder what led Tim down that path. Why would someone choose to steal from others? The question tugged at him, but he knew it wasn't his place to pry. Instead, he focused on understanding Tim's experience, hoping to learn something from his story.

As Tim's voice grew softer, his words were weighed down by the shame of his past. "We were out of control," he admitted, his eyes distant as he recalled the memory. "And the only thing that would have stopped us was getting caught."

Dean and Rose exchanged glances, their hearts pounding in anticipation. They knew Tim's story was turning darker but couldn't look away.

"Then came the day we broke into the home of someone waiting for us," Tim continued, his hands gripping the edge of his folding chair. "Turns out it was the home of a police chief."

Rose gasped, her hand flying to cover her mouth. Dean's eyes widened in shock, unable to fathom the gravity of Tim's situation. He could sense the crushing regret on the homeless man's shoulders.

"Even though we were caught red-handed, we were still upset that he had nice stuff," Tim confessed, shaking his head. His eyes met theirs, filled with vulnerability and pain. "Ever since I've been out of prison, I've felt like I don't deserve nice stuff or a nice place to lay my head after violating so many people."

As Tim's poignant words lingered in the stillness, a profound silence enveloped them, creating a charged atmosphere. It was a moment of raw, unfiltered honesty – a brave admission of guilt and shame from a man who had once lost his way as he bared his soul in a rare display of vulnerability and introspection.

In that peaceful stillness, Dean found himself reflecting on his own life. He thought about the choices he'd made, the dreams he'd pursued, and the sacrifices he'd endured. But he also recognized the importance of forgiveness and redemption for oneself and others.

"Tim," Rose said softly, her empathetic nature shining through. "You've paid your debt to society. You've served your time. You don't have to punish yourself forever."

Tim looked into her eyes, his face mixed with gratitude and disbelief. It was as if no one had ever offered him such compassion before, and Rose's words were the lifeline he'd been searching for.

"Rose is right," Dean added, touching Tim's shoulder. "You can't change the past, but you can learn from it and make better choices. You deserve a chance at happiness, just like anyone else."

As the three of them sat close together under the dim glow of the streetlights, they realized they each carried their burdens and battled their demons. Yet, as they looked at each other, they found comfort in the unspoken understanding that they were not alone in their struggles. It was a reassuring realization that they could lean on one another for support and strength.

Dean's gaze met Tim's, finding a depth of vulnerability and sincerity that belied his rough exterior.

"Tim, we can hear the remorse in your story," Dean said gently. "And if we can see it, then I'm sure God can see the remorse in your heart."

"Exactly," Rose chimed in, her eyes brimming with empathy. "You have no intention of ever returning to jail."

"Prison," Tim corrected quickly. "Not jail. They're two different situations. And I don't want to return to either one."

Rose nodded, understanding the distinction. She walked over to the cardboard box that served as Tim's makeshift home and ran her fingers along its corrugated surface, contemplating the self-imposed prison it represented. "Why put yourself in prison, then?" she asked softly.

"Everyone gets off track occasionally," she continued,

her voice steady and reassuring. "Especially when you're lost out here for too long. But we know there was something you wanted to do before all that stuff happened." She looked back at Dean, who nodded in agreement.

"Tim, you must find a way back to that. Whatever it was, you need to do it," Dean urged, his determination flaring as he imagined what it would be like to chase after long-lost dreams.

Tim's heart swelled with newfound hope at that moment – a sensation foreign to him for far too long. As he stared into the eyes of these two strangers who had offered him compassion and a chance at redemption, he realized that perhaps his life wasn't beyond repair. Maybe, just maybe, he could find his way back to the path he'd once dreamt of following.

Listening to Tim's story, they all found comfort in each other's presence, realizing that everyone faces their struggles—but no one has to confront them alone.

Then, a tremendous gust of wind rustled the leaves above them, casting dappled moonlight over Tim's worn face. He hesitated a moment before finally speaking up, his voice carrying a vulnerable, raw honesty.

"Y'know, as crazy as it may sound... I was pretty good in school, even if I pretended that I didn't like it." His eyes drifted to the stars above as if gazing into the past. "I liked learning. I wanted to be a lawyer or a teacher—something that helped people, not hurt them."

Rose and Dean exchanged glances, both touched by Tim's sincerity. It was clear that beneath the grime and hardship, there was still a spark of ambition within him, yearning to break free.

"Tim," Rose said gently, her voice soft yet firm. "Then there it is. Our work here is done. Today, we declare this is the first day of your reset, and there's no looking back."

The weight of her words seemed to settle on Tim's shoulders, a mixture of hope and fear flickering across his face. His eyes brimmed with unshed tears, and he looked down, swallowing hard.

"Thank you," he mumbled, his voice thick with emotion. "I don't know what else to say or how I'll ever repay you."

"Hey, don't worry about it," Dean said with a smile. "Just promise us you'll give it everything you've got, alright?"

"Trying is all anyone can ask for," Dean said, giving Tim's shoulder a supportive squeeze.

"Promise," Tim whispered, his determination evident in his voice.

"Good," Rose said, nodding. She glanced at Dean, who returned her gaze with understanding. It was time for them to leave Tim to his thoughts and newfound ambitions.

"Thank you for sharing your story with us, Tim," Rose said softly, her eyes shining with gratitude.

"Thank you for listening," he replied, smiling genuinely. "And remember, always be kind to yourselves and each other."

"Take care of yourself, Tim," Rose said, her hand resting briefly on his shoulder before she stepped back. "We'll see you around, okay?"

"Okay," Tim agreed, his voice wavering as he fought to keep his emotions in check. "And... thank you. Both of you."

"Of course," Dean said, clapping him on the back one last time before they turned to leave.

As they walked away, Rose couldn't help but feel a sense of warmth and pride blossoming deep within her chest. It was a small act, but it was worth every moment if it helped improve Tim's life. And as the night sky stretched above them, she knew that sometimes, even the smallest acts of kindness could create a profound difference.

Tim whispered a heartfelt "Thank you" to himself as he watched them walk away, feeling the weight of their words settle deep within him. Overwhelmed by the emotions swirling inside, he murmured, "I... I don't know where to begin, but... I'll try."

Chapter 10

The soft, rhythmic tapping of their footsteps blended seamlessly with the distant, steady hum of the city as Dean and Rose strolled side by side, each lost in their contemplative silence. The warm glow from the street-lamps cast a gentle illumination on the array of emotions that flickered and danced within their eyes, painting a poignant and intricate tableau against the urban back-drop.

As they approached the next corner of the block, the

sudden flicker of red and blue lights from a police car parked ahead immediately caught their attention. They exchanged a quick, knowing glance, silently communicating their mutual decision to continue walking straight ahead, aiming to avoid any brand-new potential complications that the presence of law enforcement might bring to their night.

"Rose," Dean began, laughter bubbling up from his chest, "I just have to say... this has been the best night of my life." He shook his head in disbelief, his eyes shining with sincerity. "Sure, it's been dangerous and eventful, but I wouldn't trade it for anything."

Puzzled, Rose raised her eyebrows, trying to decipher the meaning behind his words. "Really? But why?"

"Because it led me to you," Dean confessed, his voice soft yet unwavering. His laughter subsided, replaced by a tender smile that reached his vibrant green eyes. "Honestly, there's nothing that could top that."

Rose felt her heart skip a beat, her cheeks flushing under his gaze. Her mind raced, searching for an appropriate response, but all she could muster was a simple nod, her smile growing in response to his.

As they walked, Dean couldn't help but replay the events of the night in his head - the chaos, the fear, and the undeniable connection that had formed between them.

He knew he should be worried about the uncertainties ahead, but when he glanced at Rose, those thoughts seemed to disappear.

For the first time in a long while, Dean felt a sense of hope, like maybe fate had played its hand in bringing them together. And though he had always been one to keep his emotions bottled up, Rose had a way of drawing out his vulnerability with her gentle presence.

"Dean," Rose said softly, breaking the comfortable silence between them. "I'm happy we met tonight, too."

He grinned and squeezed her hand reassuringly, his heart swelling with gratitude for this unexpected turn of events. As they continued walking, their shadows stretching out before them, Dean knew that whatever challenges the future held, he'd face them head-on with Rose by his side.

Rose's eyes reflected its light as they widened with gratitude. "You know," she began, her words soft and sincere, "nothing like this ever happened in my small town. But then again, that town didn't have Dean Winchester. Trust me, nothing has ever topped this."

Dean's chest swelled warmly, and his eyes locked onto hers with a newfound appreciation for the woman beside him. He ran a hand through his hair, letting out a content sigh. "I'll tell you what: Let's find all the shortcuts to return to the restaurant and my car. Then, we can sit on the hood and watch the sunrise together because it'll be about that time very soon."

Rose bit her lip, excitement mingling with a hint of uncertainty as she considered his suggestion. She had never been one for spontaneous adventures, but Dean's infectious enthusiasm and genuine openness—made her want to throw caution to the wind and embrace every moment they shared.

"Alright," she agreed, nodding decisively. "Let's do it."

As they continued down the street, hand-in-hand, each step felt lighter than the last. With every whispered joke and shared secret, their connection deepened, their hearts intertwining like the shadows dancing at their feet.

Dean paused momentarily, scanning the buildings around them as he tried to recall the quickest route back to the restaurant. His mind raced, retracing their steps and attempting to piece together their winding path.

"I think I remember a shortcut just up ahead," he said, pointing towards an alleyway between two towering brick buildings.

"Lead the way," Rose replied, her voice laced with trust and anticipation.

As they ventured into the narrow passage, their footsteps echoed off the cold walls. The graffiti-covered bricks told stories of love, loss, and rebellion, mirroring the whirlwind of emotions that had brought Dean and Rose together.

"Dean," Rose murmured, her voice barely audible above their footsteps. Her eyes glistened with unshed tears as she spoke. "Thank you for showing me that there's still hope for something more than just... pain. Your kindness and support have meant the world to me."

He looked at her, his eyes glistening with empathy, and squeezed her hand. "And thank you, Rose, for reminding me that sometimes the most beautiful things in life are also the most unexpected."

They emerged from the alleyway with a shared smile and continued their journey. Their hearts were full of promise as they walked towards the impending dawn, ready to embrace the new day and its endless possibilities.

Dean and Rose stood at the edge of a small park as the first hints of morning light pierced through the gaps between buildings, casting a soft glow on the empty streets. The dew-covered grass glistened in the pale light as if to signal the dawn of a new day. In that quiet moment, they both considered what lay ahead, their intertwined hands a testament to the bond they had formed.

"Dean?" Rose asked, her voice hesitant. "What are you going to do about your living situation?"

He glanced at her, his face etched with concern. "I'm not sure yet," he admitted, his mind racing through various possibilities. "I know I can't stay where I am now, but I'll figure something out."

Rose bit her lip, her heart aching for him. She wished there was more she could do to help. "I hope it works out for you, Dean," she said softly. "You deserve so much better than life has thrown at you."

"Thanks, Rose," he replied with a warm smile that reached his eyes, making her heart flutter. "But hey, life isn't all bad. It brought me to you, right?"

She smiled back, grateful for this man who had entered her life when she needed him most. And yet, she couldn't shake a growing sense of unease, knowing that the harsh realities of life would test their newfound connection.

"Dean," she whispered, her voice trembling slightly. "I don't want this night to end, but I'm scared of the future."

"Me too," he admitted, his gaze fixed on the horizon where the sun was inching its way up into the sky. "But we'll deal with it, Rose. Whatever happens, we won't let it tear this friendship apart."

His words were like a balm to her soul, and she squeezed his hand in silent agreement. They stood there for a few moments longer, watching as the sun rose higher, its warm rays painting the world around them in shades of gold and pink.

"Let's just head back to the restaurant," Dean suggested, giving Rose's hand one last reassuring squeeze before releasing it. We'll find that shortcut I mentioned earlier."

"Alright," Rose agreed, feeling more determined than ever to face whatever challenges lay ahead with Dean.

Dean and Rose walked side by side, their shadows stretching before them as they strolled along the deserted sidewalk. The night's events were still swirling in their minds, creating excitement and apprehension that weighed heavily on their hearts.

"About my living situation," Dean began, breaking the silence between them, "I think a few people at work mentioned they were looking for roommates. I'll ask around today to get a good feel for everything." He tried to sound upbeat, but the uncertainty of his future gnawed at him.

"Sounds like a plan," Rose smiled encouragingly, her fingers brushing against his arm as they walked. She knew how difficult it was for him to open up and appreciated his honesty.

Dean glanced at her, his eyes filled with sincerity. "What about you?" he asked gently. You're going to have to face Dominic soon to deal with his cheating." At the mention of her boyfriend's name, Rose flinched, and Dean could see the pain etched on her face. He paused, put his hand on her shoulder, and offered comfort. "I'm here for you if you need me, Rose."

She looked into his eyes, seeing the genuine concern beneath his confident exterior. Her heart ached with gratitude, and she fought back tears that threatened to spill over. "Thank you, Dean," she whispered, placing her hand on his. "That means more to me than you know."

Rose found herself lost in thought as they continued walking, her mind racing with the implications of confronting Dominic. She knew it wouldn't be easy, but having Dean by her side made her feel stronger—more capable of facing the challenges ahead. She felt a flicker of hope for the first time in a long while.

"Hey," Dean said softly, drawing her out of her reverie. "Whatever happens, we'll get through this together, alright?" He lifted her hand, giving it a reassuring squeeze as they rounded the corner, the restaurant now in sight.

Rose looked up at him, her eyes shining with determination. With their fingers intertwined, they faced the morning sun, ready to confront the unknown journey that lay ahead – side by side.

"Dean," Rose started, her voice quivering slightly as she gathered the courage to share her thoughts. I've been thinking about trust, which I never truly experienced with Dominic."

His gaze was fixed on her, his eyes filled with warmth, urging her to continue.

"Tonight has shown me that there were so many lessons we've both learned. It'll take time to understand them completely." She paused, her heart pounding as the words she'd held back for so long finally found their way out. "But one thing is for sure; I never knew I was in the dark until you lit up my life."

Dean's grip on her hand tightened, but he remained silent, searching for the right words to respond. His expressive eyes reflected an emotional turmoil she hadn't expected.

"Rose," he said, his voice thick with emotion. "I've been thinking the same thing about you. You've made me see myself in a better light."

Her cheeks flushed at his admission, a mixture of joy and vulnerability flooding her senses. She admired Dean's ability to lift the spirits of those around him, but to hear that she had managed to do the same for him felt like an accomplishment beyond measure.

"Thank you," she whispered, their gazes still locked together, a silent understanding passing between them. They were two lost souls who had found solace in each other's company, and though the road ahead was uncertain, they knew they would face it side by side.

As they ventured further down the street, the sun continued ascent, casting golden rays upon the cityscape. Together, they embraced the new day, their hearts lighter and their spirits lifted by the realization that they had the power to break the cycle of broken relationships and create something beautiful together.

The morning air was tinged with a crisp coolness as it gently brushed against Rose's cheeks, bringing her back to the present. She glanced around at their surroundings, taking in the quiet street and its modest buildings.

"It's been a long night," Dean said softly, his voice barely above a whisper as he looked around, trying not to disturb the peaceful atmosphere. "Let's find somewhere to sit for a bit, catch our breath, and gather our thoughts."

He led her to an empty bus stop nearby, the metal bench offering them a place to rest and collect their thoughts. As they sat down, Dean reached over and took her hand, his fingers intertwining with hers in a silent show of support. The simple gesture filled her heart with warmth, a sensation she hadn't experienced in far too long.

"Y'know," Dean began, his gaze on their intertwined hands. "It all started at a bus stop like this hours ago. We never caught a bus, but this has been the best ride ever."

Rose couldn't help but smile, the corners of her eyes crinkling as she reflected on the night's events. It had been an emotional rollercoaster, filled with unexpected twists and turns, but she wouldn't trade it for anything.

"Life's funny that way, huh?" she mused aloud, barely above a whisper. "It takes us on these wild journeys when we least expect it."

Dean nodded, his thumb gently stroking the back of her hand. "Yeah, it does. And sometimes, those journeys lead us exactly where we need to be."

As he said those words, Rose could feel the truth of them resonating deep within her soul. She knew that whatever challenges lay ahead, she would face them head-on with Dean by her side. And in the end, that was enough.

"Thank you, Dean," she told him earnestly, her eyes locked onto his. "For everything."

His eyes shone with sincerity as he smiled back at her. "You don't have to thank me, Rose. I'm just thankful we found each other when we did."

The sun continued to rise, casting its warm glow over them as they sat in silent companionship. Each lost in their thoughts. They were bound together by the newfound connection that had blossomed between them. Though the world would soon demand their attention once more, for now, they took solace in the simplicity of a shared moment at a bus stop—two hearts forever changed by an unexpected ride.

The first full blush of dawn painted the sky in a delicate array of pinks and oranges, casting a warm glow over the quiet bus stop. As Rose took in the sight, her heart swelled with hope and newfound determination. She turned to Dean, his eyes reflecting the ethereal colors of the morning light.

"Dean," she said with conviction, "I want this ride with you to continue until the end of time."

He looked at her, his gaze tender and unwavering. The corners of his mouth lifted into a smile that reached his eyes, filling them with warmth and affection. "I'd like nothing more, Rose."

Together, they stood up, their hands still intertwined as if afraid to let go. They stepped from the bus stop, leaving behind a place similar to where their unexpected journey had begun. The world around them seemed to wake up, slowly coming to life with every step they took.

As they walked, their thoughts raced with the po-tential challenges they would face and the possibilities ahead. Rose squeezed Dean's hand reassuringly, feeling the strength of his fingers wrapped around hers. She knew they could overcome any obstacle that dared to stand in their way.

Dean could sense Rose's change, her newfound confidence and resilience shining through the vulnerability he'd witnessed earlier. It was as though she'd blossomed before his very eyes, transforming into someone who could survive the trials of life and thrive despite them.

In return, Rose recognized the subtle shift in Dean's demeanor. Beneath the ever-present smile, she could see the flicker of hope that danced in his eyes. He no longer seemed weighed down by his past struggles but instead appeared ready to embrace whatever the future held for him and them.

"Rose," Dean murmured, his voice barely above the gentle hum of the waking city, "we can do this. We can break the cycle of broken relationships and create something beautiful together."

She nodded, her eyes shining with the same conviction that filled her voice. "I have no doubt, Dean. And it all starts with trust and communication. That's how we'll make it work."

The stillness of the early morning wrapped around them like a comforting embrace, providing a momentary reprieve from the whirlwind of emotions and events that had led them to this point.

Dean's thoughts raced as he considered the enormity of their commitment to each other - a promise to break free from the shackles of their pasts and build something new and beautiful together.

A soft smile spread across Rose's lips as she glanced at their joined hands. "I can't help but feel like fate brought us together, Dean. It may have been under unusual circumstances, but we were meant to find each other."

"Me too," he confessed, his voice thick with emotion. "I never thought I'd find someone who could truly see me for who I am - and accept me, flaws and all."

"Dean, you've shown me love isn't just about the good times. It's about being there for each other during the dark moments, too," Rose said, her brown eyes shining sincerely. "And I promise you, I'll be by your side through it all."

"Thank you, Rose," Dean whispered, his heart overflowing with love, hope, and gratitude. "From now on, we are the reset we set out to be. Together."

As they neared the restaurant, their journey's starting point, the sun rose higher in the sky, illuminating a world filled with endless possibilities. Hand-in-hand, Dean, and Rose faced the challenges ahead, fortified by the knowledge that trust and communication would be the foundation of their new life together.

Chapter 11

Dean and Rose leaned against the weathered, vintage car in the restaurant's parking lot. The night had taken them through a roller coaster of emotions, and now they stood together, basking in the calm that followed the storms.

"Hey," Dean said suddenly, pushing himself off the car and walking around to the trunk. "I want to show you something." He dug around momentarily, the sound of clutter shifting, before finally pulling out his guitar.

"Here?" Rose asked, her eyes widening in surprise.

Dean smiled at her, his brown eyes twinkling with warmth, and Rose felt her heart swell in her chest. She had found solace in his presence since meeting this man who was once a stranger. She watched him cradle the guitar in his arms, running his fingers along the strings as if reuniting with an old friend.

"Listen to this," he said, strumming a few chords. His voice began to weave a gentle melody that echoed through the empty parking lot. "It's called 'It's OK.'"

As Dean sang, Rose felt herself being pulled into the music, each note resonating with a part of her soul that she thought had been long lost. The sadness that had consumed her seemed to dissipate, replaced by a sense of peace and hope. And as she looked at Dean, she saw him smiling - not just on the surface, but from deep within his core.

As the song ended, the final note lingered in the air, creating a brief but powerful moment where time seemed to stand still, and the world held its breath in anticipation of what would come next.

"When did you write that?" Rose asked, her voice barely above a whisper.

"Believe it or not," Dean replied, his gaze never leaving hers, "I wrote it the moment I saw you at that bus stop. You looked so sad, and even though I didn't know you, the music seemed to know you. It told me about you and said, 'It's OK.'"

A warm feeling spread through Rose's chest like she had been hugged from the inside. In that instant, she knew that her heart had found a safe place of refuge with Dean.

The warm glow of the sunrise stretched long across the empty parking lot. Rose leaned back against the car, her eyes locked on Dean's as he gently strummed again the last few chords of his song. A soft breeze rustled through the trees, carrying the scent of the morning dew and a promise of new beginnings.

"Dean," she said, a touch of awe in her voice, "I can't believe you still remember that song after everything we've been through tonight."

He shrugged, his fingers continuing to dance along the guitar strings absentmindedly. "It happens like that sometimes," he admitted. "I'll come up with a song I think is good but won't record it. I'll sleep on it, and if I still remember it the next day, I know it's something special." His eyes met hers again, adding, "After our long night, the song is still in my heart because it's about you, and that's what makes it special."

Rose felt her cheeks flush at his words, touched by his sincerity. She watched as he finished playing the final note again, as it lingered in the air before it was absorbed into her heart. The silence followed, punctuated only by the faint sound of birds chirping in the distance.

"Your music is amazing," she whispered, touching his arm gently. "And you can write songs like that, straight from your heart... it's incredible."

Dean smiled, setting the guitar down beside him. "Thank you, Rose." He sighed, looking up at the sky, where the first clouds had begun to appear. " I never expected to find someone who could understand my music like you. It's like you're a missing piece I didn't even know I was searching for."

As they stood side by side beneath the morning sky, Rose felt something shift inside her. The pain and sadness she had been carrying with her seemed to lessen, replaced by a sense of hope and belonging. And as she looked over at Dean, his face illuminated by the sun's soft glow, she knew they were meant to find each other.

The memory of the soft notes from his guitar still warmed her soul, and the words he had written for Rose warmed her heart.

"Thank you, Dean," she whispered, her eyes glistening with unshed tears. "When we face anything, let's remind each other that it's OK."

He nodded, the corners of his mouth lifting in a genuine smile. " Rose. We've got each other's backs now."

"That song... it was beautiful," she said, her voice barely audible. "I can't believe you wrote that just for me."

Dean chuckled, running a hand through his hair. "I've been writing songs forever because I could. It was a routine the band and I had." He paused, his gaze meeting hers. "But this was different. This was the first song that came straight from my heart, and I didn't have to look around the room for anyone's approval because this song was exactly how I felt at that moment and now."

Rose experienced an unexpected shiver that cascaded down her spine as she absorbed every syllable of his words. Each word seemed to fit together like intricate puzzle pieces, slowly revealing a breathtaking image of two individuals finding solace and profound understanding in one another amidst the relentless chaos of life. She never realized she needed this profound connection until this very moment.

"Sometimes, life throws us curveballs," she said softly, looking up at the sky. "But I think we can handle anything, right?"

"Right," Dean agreed." Silence fell between them, but it was comfortable. Each lost in their thoughts. Rose wondered what life would be like from now on with Dean by her side.

She was aware that the future held uncertainties and

challenges. Still, she found comfort in the strength of their newly formed connection, knowing that they could confront any obstacles that lay ahead with resilience and determination.

But with every challenge, they'd remind each other that it was OK and they could conquer anything as long as they had each other.

Dean's fingers danced along the frets of his guitar again, the music softly drifting through the morning air.

"Rose," Dean began, his voice barely above a whisper as he continued to pluck at the strings. "I finally understand now that my music isn't for me. It's for others, and it just happens to flow through me and will live even longer than me because I will never be the only one who feels like this, but I was the one who was meant to put it out there for those who also need it."

His eyes met hers, revealing a newfound purpose and conviction behind the familiar warmth. Dean's revelation tugged at Rose's heart, making her realize how much he'd grown in such a short amount of time.

"Dean, let me be the first to tell you that I'm one of those who needed to know. It's OK." A genuine smile spread across her face, echoing the same sentiment in her words.

He paused his playing and looked at her as if truly seeing her for the first time. The sincerity in her eyes spoke volumes, and Dean felt a surge of gratitude and love well up inside him.

"Thank you, Rose," he murmured, his fingers resuming their dance on the guitar strings, the melody more poignant than before. Dean couldn't help but think about their intertwined paths as the notes floated into the night, each step leading them closer together.

At this moment, with the world around them fading away, Dean knew they were exactly where they were meant to be. The thought brought serenity, and he found solace in the knowledge that his music could serve a greater purpose – to connect, to heal, and to remind others that they were not alone.

Dean gently and meticulously returned his cherished guitar to its place in the car, handling it as if it were the most delicate of treasures. Afterward, he carefully searched the various items in the vehicle before retrieving a soft, well-worn blanket.

"Here," he said, spreading the blanket across the car's hood. "Let's lay down and enjoy this beautiful morning for a while."

They climbed onto the hood, lying side by side, their shoulders touching as they gazed at the heavens above them. The scent of dewy grass still fills the air, mingling with the faint aroma of car exhaust, creating a strangely comforting blend of nature and humanity.

"Dean?" Rose's voice was hesitant, her words slowly drifting into the heavens like a tentative question mark. "What if we never met yesterday? What in the world would we be doing right now?"

He chuckled softly, the sound warm and genuine. "Well, I'd probably be sleeping somewhere in the back of my car with this same blanket we're on right now."

His casual response brought a smile to her face. She imagined a scruffy, tousle-haired Dean curled up in the cramped space of his car, seeking solace in his music even when alone. A strangely endearing image made her feel an even deeper connection to him.

"Hey, don't laugh," he teased, lightly nudging her shoulder. "Sometimes the best inspiration comes from the strangest places."

Rose nodded, understanding that beneath his playful demeanor, Dean took his passion seriously. She could almost feel the weight of his dreams and aspirations in the quiet moments between them as though they were hers. She wondered if he ever felt the same about her hopes and fears.

"Whatever path life had taken us on, I'm glad it led us here," she murmured, her words carrying the sincerity of a heartfelt prayer. "I can't imagine facing all the challenges without you by my side."

Dean's hand hesitated momentarily before finding its way to hers, their fingers intertwining as naturally as the harmonies in his music. "Me neither, Rose. Me neither."

As they lay there, wrapped in the warmth of each other's presence and lost in their thoughts, the world seemed to slow down just for them, allowing them to savor every heartbeat and whispered word. And with every breath, Dean and Rose drew closer to the truth that they were meant to be – two souls bound together by a shared understanding of life's fragile beauty and the healing power of love.

The sun's golden rays gently caressed Rose's face, creating a warm and enchanting glow as she gazed up at the vast expanse of the sky, her eyes filled with a captivating sense of awe and curiosity.

Overwhelmed by a deep understanding of love and admiration for the woman by his side, Dean found himself utterly captivated by the sight of her. At that moment, he couldn't help but ponder whether she genuinely comprehended her profound impact on his life in such a remarkably brief period.

"Rose," he began cautiously, not wanting to disturb the serenity that enveloped them. "What do you think you'd be doing now if we hadn't met?"

She hesitated, her fingers absently playing with the edge of the blanket beneath them. "Honestly? I don't know if I'd even be here right now," she admitted, her voice barely above a whisper. "I don't know what I was thinking with those pills."

Dean's heart clenched at her words. The thought of losing her, of never having had the chance to know her, made his chest tighten with an unbearable weight. He reached over and gently squeezed her hand, a silent reminder that he was there for her.

"Hey," he said softly, his gaze locked on hers. "Let's not go back there, alright? God had a bigger plan for you; deep down inside, you knew it. You just had no idea it would include someone like me."

Rose laughed, a sound both fragile and genuine. "Someone like you?" She echoed. "You mean someone amazing, talented, and caring? Yeah, you're right – I never would have guessed."

Dean felt a warmth spread through him at her words. His insecurities often threatened to drown him, but with Rose by his side, he was buoyed by her unwavering faith in him. It amazed him how she saw him – not just as a struggling busboy with dreams of making music but as a person worthy of love and happiness.

"Maybe it's fate," he mused, his mind racing with their

future possibilities together. "Or maybe it's just a beautiful coincidence that brought us together. Whatever it is, I'm grateful for it."

"Me too," Rose whispered, her eyes glistening with unshed tears. "More than words can say."

Dean couldn't help but marvel at his life's extraordinary turn. It was as if the universe had conspired to bring them together – two kindred spirits who understood each other's pain and dreams with a depth that transcended time and circumstance.

As the day brightened around them, cloaking them in a blanket of clouds and sunlight, they reveled in the quiet assurance that whatever today held for them would be OK. They would face it together, hand in hand and heart to heart.

"Last night was... incredible," Rose said softly, her voice barely more than a whisper as she stared at the sky. "Meeting you, talking, laughing, crying – it's been the best part of my night. From now on, I will continue to wait on the Lord with newfound strength and resilience."

Dean's chest swelled with warmth at her words. He couldn't help but reflect on how much had changed in just a matter of hours. How this beautiful, vulnerable woman had come into his life like a beacon of light, illuminating the shadows that had once consumed him.

"Maybe we should revisit Pastor Dave's church some-time," he suggested, his tone contemplative. That level of peace we felt there seems to improve us at life, you know?"

Rose turned her head slightly, her eyes meeting his, filled with gratitude and understanding. "I'd like that," she agreed, her smile lighting up her face like the first rays of the morning sun. "I think we both need that calming presence in our lives."

Dean Winchester finally understood what it meant to be truly alive.

"Sometimes, it felt like Pastor Dave's words had a way of reaching right into your soul, didn't it?" Rose mused, her voice barely more than a whisper as she traced the outline of a constellation with her finger.

Dean nodded, closing his eyes momentarily as he allowed the memory of their time at the church to wash over him. "It's like he knew exactly what we needed to hear," he replied, opening his eyes to find Rose smiling softly. "And somehow, those words stayed with us, guiding us through our darkest moments."

"Speaking of which," Rose said with a gentle nudge of her elbow, "remember when you told me that we should remind each other that it's OK? Let's do that now." She turned to face him fully, her eyes searching his for an unspoken understanding.

"OK" was a simple word, but it held so much weight and meaning when spoken between them. It reminded them of the bond they'd forged, a testament to their resilience and the healing power of love.

"Everything will be OK. Rose," Dean assured her, his smile tender and genuine as he squeezed her hand. "No matter what life throws at us, we'll get through it together."

"OK," Rose echoed, her eyes shimmering with unshed tears of gratitude and relief. They gazed at each other momentarily, letting the truth of their shared promise sink in.

Once battered and bruised by life's storms, their hearts are beat with renewed hope and purpose.

A quiet understanding took root in that sacred space between them—an unspoken vow. Dean and Rose finally understood what it meant to be at peace.

Chapter 12

The cool metal beneath them hummed with the residual warmth of the engine, mirroring the comforting heat that radiated from their connected hands. Everything felt peaceful, as if the world had paused just for them.

"Hey, look who's here!" A familiar voice broke through their bubble.

Startled, they glanced up to see some of their co-workers arriving at the restaurant, their faces a mixture of confusion and delight. They exchanged smirks, knowing their new relationship would be the day's talk.

"Looks like you guys had one heck of a night! You ended up back at work, huh?" one of their colleagues teased, winking at them.

Dean chuckled, pulling Rose to her feet as he hopped off the car's hood. Hand in hand, they walked towards the entrance, where the manager greeted them with a smile.

"Good morning, you two," he said, his eyes twinkling with excitement. "Since you're both here already, why don't you come inside? It's going to be a beautiful day."

"Sure thing, boss," Dean replied, grinning back at him. Rose smiled shyly, her cheeks tinged pink with embarrassment and happiness.

As they stepped through the doors of the elegant restaurant, their colleagues couldn't contain their curiosity and began to inquire about their blossoming romance. It seemed almost surreal, considering that Rose had only started her role as a hostess the day before. The glint of intrigue in their eyes was unmistakable, as they were eager to uncover the story behind this unexpectedly rapid connection.

Dean found himself standing in the bustling prep area of the restaurant, surrounded by the clatter of pots and pans. Glancing around, he sensed his colleagues' palpable curiosity and anticipation.

They were all eager to unravel the enigma surrounding his connection with Rose. Despite feeling hesitant, Dean knew he needed to find the perfect words to convey the profound significance of their encounter. Taking a moment to collect his thoughts, he drew a deep breath and finally began sharing the story.

"You never know where your blessing will come from," he said softly, his voice taking on a certain poetic quality as if recounting a life-changing moment he'd never forget. His eyes sparkled with sincerity as he continued, "Mine came from watching a beautiful lady sitting at a bus stop who looked like she needed someone to tell her that it would be OK. So that's what I did, and the rest is history."

As Dean's words resonated throughout the room, the atmosphere shifted. A hushed silence replaced the laughter and chatter that had filled the space before as everyone listened intently. It was as if they were all pausing to reflect on the precious moments when kindness had transformed their lives.

Rose gazed at him, her eyes shining with admiration and gratitude. She squeezed his hand gently, overwhelmed by the depth of their connection in such a short time.

"Wow," one co-worker breathed, clearly touched by Dean's words. "That's something."

As they went about their tasks, their colleagues couldn't help but steal glances at the pair, marveling at the unexpected bond that had formed between them. They witnessed the birth of an authentic, heartfelt, and engaging love story. The tale made people believe in the power of love and fate.

Dean's eyes met Rose's briefly, and their shared memories flooded back to them: the bustling city street, Dean hurrying to work on a day when he was facing eviction, and this woman, lost in thought, waiting for a bus. But at that moment, Dean saw something in her that others may have missed. He saw someone who needed a kind word, a gesture of support.

The impact of that small act of kindness rippled out in unexpected ways. There were cheers and laughter in the prep area of the restaurant where Dean worked. His story would inspire others to spread kindness and seek opportunities to make a difference. It was a powerful reminder that sometimes, the greatest blessings come from simple acts of kindness.

"Thank you for sharing that with us, Dean," another co-worker said, her eyes glistening with unshed tears. "It's amazing how a simple gesture can change everything."

Dean smiled and nodded, appreciating his colleagues' support and understanding. As he turned to look at Rose, he knew that their journey had only just begun. But one thing was sure: together, they would continue to spread kindness and love, creating ripples of change that would touch the lives of those around them.

"Here's to new beginnings," Dean whispered to Rose, and she smiled back, knowing that this was only the start of something beautiful and everlasting.

Rose couldn't help but be captivated by the sincerity in his eyes, feeling her heart swell with affection for the man who had pulled her from the depths of despair.

"Thank you," she whispered, almost too soft to be heard over their colleagues' clatter of dishes and laughter. She knew how vulnerable Dean must have been to share their story with the others, and she appreciated that he spared them both the more painful details. Their connection was still so new and delicate—something to be cherished and nurtured privately before sharing it entirely with the world.

With Dean finished speaking, Rose took a moment to gather her thoughts, feeling the weight of gratitude settle in her chest. Her reverie was interrupted when one of her co-workers, a fellow hostess named Lily, gently tugged on her arm and pulled her to the side.

"Hey, Rose," Lily began, her voice filled with warmth. "I just wanted to say I'm so happy to see this new glow on your face. When you returned to work yesterday, you looked like you were carrying the world's weight on your shoulders. But today, you seem lighter, somehow. I didn't want to pry since you were new, but I'm glad things are looking up for you."

Rose smiled softly at Lily's words, touched by her concern and understanding. "Thank you. Today, my life has reset. It feels like everything is finally falling into place."

Lily grinned, her eyes sparkling with happiness for her new friend. "Well, you go with your reset self. I'm happy for you."

"Thanks, Lily," Rose replied, her cheeks flushed with gratitude. As Lily returned to her duties, Rose glanced back at Dean, who was now conversing with another busboy. Her fingertips brushed against the pendant resting on her chest, a tangible reminder of their connection and the healing power of love.

"Here's to new beginnings," Rose thought, feeling the strength of her newfound happiness surge through her veins. Life had been cruel and unforgiving, but in the warmth of Dean's embrace and the kindness of her co-workers, she had found solace – and a reason to keep moving forward.

Dean's eyes scanned the room, taking in the vibrant energy of his co-workers as they prepared for the day ahead.

He felt a warmth deep within him, knowing he had contributed to creating this atmosphere of camaraderie and kindness. Just as he was about to return to his duties, a fellow busboy, Tom, sidled up to him with an amused grin.

"Best man won, huh?" Tom said, clapping Dean on the back.

"Sorry, what?" Dean furrowed his brow in confusion.

"Rose," Tom clarified, gesturing towards her across the room. "I had my eye on her since she started yesterday. I thought she was nice, you know? But you beat me to the punch."

Dean's heart swelled with pride and protectiveness and a quiet understanding that fate had played its part in bringing them together. His voice softened as he responded, "Even if you'd made a move, Tom, it wouldn't have mattered. Sometimes things are just meant to be, and they're out of our control."

Tom nodded, a touch nostalgic but accepting. "Yeah, I get that. Life has a weird way of working itself out sometimes."

With a final pat on the shoulder, Tom left Dean to his thoughts. It wasn't long before Dean remembered something he'd overheard earlier. Approaching another co-worker, Emily, he broached the subject tentatively.

"Hey, Emily, I heard you were looking for a roommate?"

Emily glanced up from the tray she was arranging, her eyes clouding with sympathy. "Oh, Dean, I'm so sorry. We already found someone last night."

"That's alright," Dean replied, forcing a smile despite the disappointment gnawing at the edges of his newfound happiness. "I'll figure something out. My band broke up yesterday, so I'll need a place to stay."

"Again, I'm sorry," Emily said, her gaze filled with genuine concern. "I hope you find something soon."

"Thanks, Emily. I appreciate it," Dean murmured, his mind racing with the practicalities of finding a new home amidst the whirlwind of emotions that had engulfed him in the past twenty-four hours.

As he continued with his tasks, Dean couldn't help but reflect on the unpredictable nature of life - how moments of profound joy could coexist with heartache and uncertainty and how the people who entered our lives could shape our destinies in ways we never imagined. He glanced over at Rose, her radiant smile a beacon in the chaos of the kitchen, and knew without a doubt that he would face whatever challenges lay ahead with courage, resilience, and an open heart.

The scent of freshly brewed coffee mingled with the aroma of sizzling bacon and pancakes, enveloping Dean in a warm embrace as he navigated the bustling kitchen.

His thoughts drifted back to the tender moments he had shared with Rose earlier that morning, their hearts intertwining beneath the vast expanse of the sky.

"Dean," the manager called out, his voice pulling Dean from his reverie. "I heard about your band breaking up. I'm sorry, man."

"Thanks, Mr. Thompson," Dean replied, his heart heavy with losing a dream he had held for so long. I appreciate it. You've always been supportive, even coming to our gigs."

Mr. Thompson's eyes glinted with genuine empathy. "You guys were great; it's a shame it had to end."

Dean sighed, nodding in agreement. "Yeah, it's disappointing. I'm not sure what's next for me musically."

"Actually," Mr. Thompson said, leaning conspiratorially, "I might have something for you. My friend's getting married soon, and they're looking for someone to perform at the wedding. I told them about you. How'd you feel about doing it?"

"Really?" Dean hesitated, contemplating the possibility. Could he do it alone? He took a deep breath, acknowledging the flicker of excitement that ignited within him. " I've been working on some new material that might be perfect for a wedding lately."

"Fantastic!" Mr. Thompson clapped him on the back,

his enthusiasm contagious. "I'll pass along your contact info to my friend. I'm sure they'll be thrilled."

"Thank you, Mr. Thompson," Dean said, his gratitude blooming like a flower in his chest. This opportunity presented a chance to prove that he could shine, even without his band. "I won't let you down."

Dean's mind buzzed with ideas for the wedding performance as he returned to his tasks. He envisioned himself on stage, pouring his heart into the music, captivating the audience with every note. It was a new beginning, a chance to redefine himself as an artist.

Amid the kitchen chaos, Dean found solace in the thought that life presented unexpected opportunities. Glancing over at Rose, her presence a testament to the beauty of vulnerability and connection, he felt sure they could navigate whatever challenges.

Rose's eyes stung as she sliced through the onions, her hands moving with practiced precision. Her colleagues beside her murmured their complaints about the pungent smell, but Rose suddenly felt a wave of self-consciousness wash over her. It had been a long night and an even longer morning, and she couldn't shake the feeling that the unpleasant odor lingering around her might not be entirely due to the onions.

"Hey," she whispered to her co-worker, Carina, who

diced onions. "Do you think this smell comes from me, or is it just the onions?"

Carina paused momentarily. Her brow furrowed in concentration as she took a cautious sniff. She hesitated before responding, her voice gentle and apologetic. "I thi nk... well, it's not just the onions."

"Thanks for being honest," Rose sighed, her cheeks flushed with embarrassment. "I'll go home and change my clothes." She wiped her hands on her apron, untied it, and hung it up before stepping out of the prep area to search for Dean.

As she navigated the bustling restaurant, she spotted him by the bar, conversing with another employee. Rose approached slowly, not wanting to interrupt, and waited nearby, observing him from a distance. Despite his challenges, Dean seemed to carry an air of confidence, his smile unwavering as he spoke animatedly about his music. Rose couldn't help but admire his resilience, especially considering the recent dissolution of his band.

While she waited, her thoughts drifted to the events of last night and this morning, the emotional rollercoaster they had shared. She felt renewed hope and a blossoming affection for Dean, her heart swelling with gratitude for his support and understanding. She glanced at the simple silver bracelet he had given her from out of his car earlier.

She couldn't help but smile, her heart aching with the beauty of their newfound connection.

"Dean," she called softly when his conversation lulled. He turned to face her, his eyes lighting up at the sight of her.

"Rose?" Dean's voice cut through her thoughts as he approached her, his brow furrowed in concern. "You, OK?"

"Yeah," she replied, attempting a smile. I have to go home, shower, and change my clothes."

"Of course," he said softly, understanding the reason behind her request. He hesitated momentarily, adding, "Do you want me to come with you?"

The offer, spoken with such earnest sincerity, tugged at her heartstrings. She momentarily imagined how comforting it would be to have him by her while confronting the memories of Dominic's betrayal. But then, a steely resolve surged within her, reminding her that some battles were meant to be fought alone.

"No, I can manage," she assured him, trying to infuse confidence into her words. "But thank you, Dean. You have no idea how much that means to me."

His smile returned, softening the worry lines on his face. "Anything for you, Rose. I'm just a phone call away if you need me, alright?"

"Alright." She met his gaze, marveling at the warmth and

compassion shimmering in his eyes. It was like staring into a pool of molten gold filled with promises of comfort and solace.

"Go on, take care of yourself. We'll be here when you get back," Dean encouraged her, gently squeezing her shoulder before letting go.

Dean nodded solemnly, understanding the gravity of her words. The tangled web that Dominic had woven now lay in shambles at her feet, and it was up to her to pick up the broken pieces. It wasn't an easy task, but it was one she knew she needed to face head-on.

"Take your time," he assured her, his hand brushing against hers briefly before she turned to leave. The fleeting touch sent a jolt of electricity through her veins, a reminder of their shared connection.

For a moment, their gazes locked, and Rose felt as if she were standing on the edge of a precipice, teetering between the life she had known and the uncertain future that awaited her. Dean's presence was like an anchor, grounding her amidst the stormy seas of change.

"I appreciate you, Dean Winchester," she whispered, her words carrying the weight of all her unspoken gratitude. "I'll be right back."

"Thank you," she whispered, her voice catching in her throat. Rose turned and headed for the door with one last glance at him, her heart swelling with renewed hope in the face of adversity.

Rose hesitated, her fingers hovering above the door handle. "I have to handle this part alone," she said softly, drawing strength from within. "It wouldn't be fair even though he brought another woman into my apartment, and then I turned around and did the same thing with bringing Dean."

As she stepped out into the crisp morning air, Rose took a deep breath, filling her lungs with the sweet scent of new beginnings. With each stride towards her apartment, she left the past behind, inch by inch, determined to forge a new path for herself—one where happiness and love were no longer distant dreams but tangible realities.

A quiet revolution stirred inside her heart, fueled by the unwavering belief that she deserved better than the pain that had once held her captive. And with Dean by her side, she knew that anything was possible.

"Alright," she murmured, summoning every ounce of courage. Let's do this."

And with that, Rose Evans turned the key, unlocking the door to her home and the promise of a brighter tomorrow.

Chapter 13

Rose, a woman of delicate strength, felt her fingers tremble as she turned the rusted key in the lock. The harsh, grating sound of metal scraping against metal reverberated in the dimly lit hallway's eerie stillness, sending shivers down her spine. She paused, her heart pounding so loudly in her chest that she was sure it could be heard throughout the building before summoning every ounce of courage to slowly push the heavy door open.

Her mind was filled with fear and anticipation, akin

to cautiously entering a long-abandoned, haunted house. The once-familiar scent of lavender, which had always been so comforting, now carried a bitter undertone of betrayal, causing her to inhale sharply as a wave of sadness washed over her.

Memories engulfed her as she cautiously crossed the threshold into the apartment. The walls seemed to echo with the laughter they once shared, the whispered confidences, and the shared aspirations for the future. However, those dreams now lay in ruins, shattered by Dominic's betrayal. The image of him entwined with another woman was seared into her mind, sending more palpable shivers down her spine.

"Breathe," Rose reminded herself through gritted teeth, feeling her chest tighten with anxiety. She stood with her back on the closed door, its solid barrier offering respite from the outside chaos. As she shut out the world, she focused on slowing down her racing thoughts, giving herself the space she needed to gather her emotions and find a sense of calm within.

But as she sank onto the worn, overstuffed couch, tears flowed uncontrollably down her cheeks. The weight of her sorrow pressed heavily on her chest as she grappled with the realization that she had been so blind. How did she not see Dominic care only about his dreams, leaving hers in the dust?

"I deserve better," Rose muttered, her voice trembling with a mixture of sadness and anger as she wiped away her tears. But amidst the overwhelming emotions, a small, bittersweet smile tugged at the corners of her lips when she thought of Dean.

Amid her pain and despair, he had been a beacon of light, bringing warmth and hope into her life when everything seemed dark and impossible. His unwavering belief in her and his steadfast support had been a source of strength, giving her the courage to envision a brighter, more hopeful future.

"Dean," she whispered with gratitude, feeling a weight lift off her chest ever so slightly. It was a relief to have someone to lean on in her time of need. But then guilt crept in as she remembered he was just a friend. Despite understanding that their relationship was strictly platonic, she couldn't help but feel his unwavering support was unique and fresh, especially in contrast to Dominic's absence during any of her difficult times.

As Rose gazed around her cozy apartment, her eyes landed on each familiar object, evoking memories and emotions. This space was not just a place to live; it was her sanctuary, a testament to her hard work and resilience. At this moment, a powerful surge of determination filled her being. She realized that it was time to take back control of her life and pursue her dreams, unshackled from the expectations of others.

While the memories and emotions of the past still lingered, they no longer held her captive. With newfound strength, she felt ready to embrace the unknown and carve out her future, whatever it may have.

Rose stood by the living room window. Her eyes fixated on the intricate patterns the raindrops cascading down the glass formed. Each droplet seemed to reflect her inner turmoil and confusion as it hesitated before joining forces with others and descending in unison.

After taking a deep breath, she tore her gaze away from the window and shifted her attention to the weathered coffee table, a steadfast presence in her life for countless years.

"Can you believe the time we were playing that intense game during game night, and you were laughing so hard that you accidentally knocked over your glass of red wine, spilling it all over this table?" she whispered, a mix of fondness and bitterness in her voice. It had been one of the many joyous moments she had shared with Dominic, but now it felt tarnished by the sense of betrayal she had recently uncovered.

"Rose constantly repeated the mantra "Focus on the

good" to banish the negative thoughts and emotions threatening to overwhelm her. Her apartment was a minefield of memories, each item representing a different moment in her tumultuous relationship with Dominic.

A bittersweet wave of emotions washed over her as she gazed at a framed photograph capturing their radiant smiles during a vacation in Italy. "We were so carefree and happy then," she murmured, her fingers delicately tracing the frame's contours. "But even amidst such beauty, we couldn't escape the pain that followed."

As Rose sauntered towards her bedroom, her mind was filled with Dean's comforting words from earlier: "You're strong, Rose. You'll get through this." His reassuring voice echoed in her thoughts, offering hope amid the whirlwind of emotions.

"Dean," she whispered, her voice barely audible as she clung to his unwavering support, feeling an overwhelming gratitude. Despite his encouraging words, Rose could not dispel the persistent doubt and fear that relentlessly gnawed at her.

Rose carefully sifted through her neatly arranged clothes in the serene ambiance of her bedroom closet in search of some particular items. As her fingers trailed along the fabric, they finally landed on two beautifully wrapped boxes concealed behind a line of elegant dresses.

As she cradled them close to her heart, a flood of memories washed over her, reminding her of the care and love she had poured into selecting these perfect gifts for Dominic. However, these once cherished tokens of affection now served as painful mementos of his unfaithfulness.

"Should I even bother giving these to him?" she pondered, her mind torn between holding on to what they had and letting go of the pain he had caused her. As she sat in her dimly lit room, surrounded by memories of happier times, Rose couldn't help but feel conflicted. Despite the hurt and betrayal, a part of her still cared deeply for Dominic. However, she also knew she couldn't continue letting his actions dictate her emotions.

With a heavy heart, she made a decision. "This is enough," she whispered, placing the carefully wrapped boxes back in their hiding spot. "It's time to focus on myself and my happiness. It's time to prioritize my dreams and well-being over the lingering attachment to someone who doesn't deserve my love."

And with that, Rose took a deep breath, feeling empowered as she embraced the beginning of a new chapter in her life.

Rose gazed at the walls, holding countless joyful and painful memories as she stood in her apartment. She recognized that delving into a process of introspection and personal development would present challenges, but she understood it was an essential step toward progress.

"Here's to a new beginning," she whispered, ready to face whatever challenges life had in store for her next.

Rose's hands trembled as she returned to retrieve and put the gift-wrapped boxes into a large, unassuming bag. With each item she carefully placed inside, her heart twisted in agony. How could she even think of giving these gifts to him after what he had done? As she finished, an unpleasant stench assaulted her senses, causing her to gag and stumble backward.

The smell was a mix of old sweat and onions as if they had been rotting under her arms for a long time. It made her feel even more uneasy about her life situation, intensifying her internal struggle.

"Her stomach churned with disgust as she muttered under her breath, raising a shaking hand to cover her nose. The realization of how low she had sunk hit her hard as she had again allowed herself to be fooled by his empty promises.

Fueled to rid herself of any reminder of him, she stormed to the front door with purpose and placed the bag next to the door, the weight of her decision settling heavily in the air."

Dominic sat in his old, weathered sedan parked across

the street from Rose's apartment building. The tears streamed down his face as he gazed at the apartment's windows. His heart ached with longing and regret, and his fingers tapped anxiously against the worn leather of the steering wheel.

He knew his thoughtless actions had caused her deep pain, and now, as he sat in silence, he mustered the courage to face her. His mind raced with thoughts of how he could make things right and win back her love, knowing the road ahead would be complex and uncertain.

"You have to do this," he reminded himself, trying to drown out the voice that told him it was too late for them. "You need to show her you're not just another mistake she believes she's made."

But with each passing minute, his hope began to falter. His mistakes weighed heavy on his shoulders, threatening to crush any chance of reconciliation with Rose.

"I don't deserve her," he thought bitterly as he watched her move around her apartment. "But I have to try."

Rose sighed heavily inside the apartment and slowly peeled off her clothes, each piece feeling heavier than the last as it hit the floor. The warm steam enveloped her as she stepped into the shower, and she closed her eyes, letting the hot water cascade over her body.

The pounding water felt like a temporary relief, as if it

could wash away the physical pain and emotional turmoil that consumed her. But no matter how hard she scrubbed, she couldn't rid herself of the betrayal and doubt that plagued her mind, lingering like an unshakeable shadow.

"Can I forgive him?" she wondered as she closed her eyes and let the water envelop her. Despite wanting to believe in a future where they could start over, she couldn't silence the nagging voice of doubt whispered in her ear.

Dominic and Rose were both lost in their thoughts as the water continued to flow, grappling with the same question: Was their love strong enough to overcome the pain and mistrust that had torn them apart? And as they searched for an answer, their hearts clenched with the realization that what lay ahead was uncertain and terrifying.

But deep inside, they both held onto a glimmer of hope—that maybe, just maybe, love would find a way to heal their broken relationship.

The water cascaded down Rose's face, a fierce storm of tears mingling with the relentless spray from the showerhead. Each drop felt like a dagger, piercing her skin and washing away the remnants of her broken past. Her heart throbbed painfully, but she found solace in the water's comforting warmth.

With her eyes tightly shut, she took a deep breath, steeling herself to let go of the pain and move on. But then, a familiar sound shattered her brief moment of peace—the creaking of the bathroom door being slowly pushed open. Instantly, Rose's haven was tainted by a sense of vulnerability.

"Who's there?" she called out, her voice quivering with fear.

"Welcome home, baby," came Dominic's smooth reply as he stepped into the bathroom, completely naked. His attempt at a reassuring smile faltered under Rose's intense stare.

Anger coursed through her veins like a raging river, drowning out lingering traces of fear. With a deep breath, she turned off the shower's cascading water and reached for the plush towel, wrapping it tightly around her trembling form.

The once serene ambiance of the room was now thick with an oppressive silence as Rose strode past Dominic, her eyes flashing with unspoken fury.

Rose methodically chose her clothes in her bedroom as if each decision were a critical life choice. Her movements were precise and calculated, masking the turmoil raging inside her. Just as she slipped on her blouse, Dominic appeared in the doorway.

"Welcome home, baby," he repeated his earlier words, desperately trying to warm his tone.

Rose shot back with venom dripping from every word, "Just get dressed and tell your new friend she left something behind."

Dominic's face flushed with shame as he scrambled to put on his clothes. "Rose, I messed up, but we can fix this. Remember our dreams? We were supposed to conquer the world together."

But Rose glared back at him coldly, her eyes filled with pure disgust. This look cut him deep, making him realize the gravity of his mistake. No apology or promises of a bright future could erase the hurt and betrayal he had caused.

"Do you think that's enough?" Rose's voice shook with rage. "That I'll forgive you just because you say sorry and remind me of our dreams? You have no idea what you've done."

Dominic opened his mouth to speak, but no words came out. The pain in his eyes mirrored the realization that he may have lost her forever.

With a sharp inhale, Rose musters up all her courage and steps out of the bedroom, steeling herself for another confrontation with Dominic. But fate seems to have other plans as she collides with him in the doorway, their bodies slamming together like two ships in a violent storm.

The tension between them crackles like electricity, a palpable force threatening to explode at any moment.

"Rose," Dominic begins, his voice thick with emotions he can't quite name. "We need to talk. Listen and be heard."

She avoids his gaze, her eyes fixed on the empty kitchen table, which beckons to her like a lifeline. She grabs a pen and paper, ready to spill her heart onto the page. "Go ahead," she mutters, not daring to look up from her task. "Talk."

Dominic hesitates, struggling to find the right words to bridge their chasm. He wants nothing more than to make things right but knows it won't be easy. With each passing moment, the rift between them seems to grow wider, threatening to swallow him whole.

"Where were you all night?" he finally asks, hoping that showing genuine concern for her well-being might help bring them closer together. "I was worried about you."

Rose's hand freezes on the page, her grip on the pen tightening as she processes the audacity of his question. Slowly, she turns to face him, her expression unreadable and her eyes narrowed in suspicion.

For a brief moment, Dominic glimpses a flicker of pain behind her icy facade – a silent reminder of the hurt he has caused.

"That's what you're worried about?" she asks incredulously. "Whether I'll come back? Or if your little side piece will see who you are?"

Without waiting for an answer, she turns away from him and resumes writing with a newfound determination. Dominic stands there, the weight of his mistakes crushing him as he struggles to find the right words.

"Rose," he whispers desperately, reaching out for her but falling short. "Please, I just want to make things right."

But Rose knows that some wounds run too deep to heal completely – and sometimes, the only way to move forward is to leave the past behind and start anew.

Dominic's throat constricted painfully as he watched Rose's pen slash across the page, his heart racing like a runaway train. A deep-seated panic took hold of him, threatening to consume his entire being. He couldn't bear the thought of her leaving, of losing her forever.

"Rose, please," he gasped, desperation lacing his words.

But she ignored him, continuing to write with fierce determination. The sound of the pen scratching against paper was deafening in the small apartment, a cruel reminder of what was slipping away from him.

In a moment of recklessness, Dominic lunged forward and snatched the letter from her hands. He desperately hoped that reading her words would give him insight into her thoughts, some way to change her mind.

"Give that back!" Rose snapped, fury blazing in her eyes.

"Just let me see, Rose," he pleaded, scanning the letter frantically. Each word felt like a dagger to his heart: a scathing letter addressed to him and their landlord, declaring her intention for Dominic to leave because of their troubled relationship. She was giving them notice for Dominic to vacate the apartment by the end of the day.

"Is this how you want things to end?" Dominic asked shakily, tears welling in his eyes. "We can work through this."

But she shook her head firmly. "That letter is my final decision, Dominic. I won't change my mind. You and your... partner can continue whatever you do somewhere else."

"Proper notice should be given, Rose," he argued weakly, feeling like his world was crumbling around him.

"This is my proper notice," she replied coldly, refusing to meet his gaze any longer. "Consider this the end."

"Rose, please," he begged, feeling like he was drowning in heartache. But deep down, he knew it was futile – their relationship was over, and the weight of that realization threatened to crush him.

"This is Goodbye, Dominic," she whispered, her voice barely audible. With those final, gut-wrenching words, Rose Evans definitively closed the door on their life together in her heart, leaving behind both her love and her pain, the weight of her decision palpable in the air.

Heavy and suffocating silence hung between them like a dense fog, smothering any hope of reconciliation. Dominic's face contorted with a maelstrom of emotions – anger, desperation, and heartbreak – as his eyes desperately scanned Rose's, seeking a glimmer of hope in the abyss.

Her body, a canvas of unspoken words, revealed the depth of her inner turmoil. Once open and inviting, her posture now stood rigid and defensive, a silent testament to the pain she was trying to hide.

Rose turned away, determined not to be swayed by the vulnerability in his gaze. She fixed her gaze on a distant point, steeling herself when a soft, ominous knock shattered the tense stillness. Their hearts skipped a beat as they flinched at the sound, their eyes darting towards the door in unison, their breaths caught in their throats.

With a bitter edge to her voice, Rose murmured, "Your partner probably thought I wouldn't come back. You should answer the door and tell her you're free now."

Dominic hesitated, his hand hovering over the doorknob, torn between his conflicting emotions. His fingers flexed and unflexed nervously as he struggled to decide whether opening that door would bring salvation or more pain—the room filled with a heavy, anticipatory silence.

"Go ahead," Rose urged softly, barely above a whisper. "It's over, Dominic. It doesn't matter." The finality in her tone made him cringe.

It was time for her to turn the page and start a new chapter in her life, one where she would carve her path and chase after her dreams. And though the road ahead was uncertain and daunting, Rose knew she was ready to face whatever challenges came her way, her determination shining through the uncertainty.

The door loomed before Dominic like an impenetrable fortress, its heavy presence casting a dark shadow over his guilt-ridden face. His hand trembled as he attempted to reach for the doorknob again, a knot of fear tightening in his stomach at the thought of what lay beyond.

Rose stood by his side, her eyes darting between his anguished expression and the daunting door. Despite everything that had transpired, her heart ached for him. "Hey," she whispered, placing a comforting hand on his arm. "I'll open it."

With a deep breath, Rose twisted the doorknob and determinedly flung the door open. She gasped in surprise when she saw Dean standing on the other side, his brow furrowed with concern. The sight of him brought a wave of relief crashing over her.

"Rose?" Dean's voice was worried as he took in her

tear-stained face. "What happened? Are you okay?"

A solitary tear escaped Rose's eye, and she nodded, a small smile spreading across her lips. "I am now."

Dominic's curiosity was piqued by the sight of Rose's awestruck expression beside Dean. He took a step forward, eyeing the newcomer suspiciously. "Who is this?" he demanded, struggling to keep his voice steady.

Dean met Dominic's gaze head-on, his tone unwavering and protective of Rose. "You don't want me to be your problem, man."

Fists clenched at his sides, Dominic couldn't deny the truth in Dean's words. He looked at Rose and saw something new in her – a glimmer of hope, of strength. And suddenly, he knew that their time together had ended.

"Fine," Dominic grumbled, shoulders slumping in defeat. He stepped back, allowing Dean and Rose to face whatever lay ahead without him.

As the door closed behind Dominic, Rose felt the weight of her past begin to lift from her shoulders. She knew the road ahead wouldn't be easy, but with Dean by her side, she was ready to face it. Together, they would forge a new path built on trust, understanding, and a love that could withstand even the darkest storms.

Chapter 14

The room was aglow with a soft, warm light emanating from the gentle hum of a single table lamp. Its golden rays cast delicate, dancing shadows across the walls, creating an atmosphere of tranquility.

Rose sat nestled on the couch, her tear-streaked face catching the glimmer of the dim light. Her body trembled with silent sobs as she fought to regain her composure.

Dean sat beside Rose, his arm wrapped around her shoulders, offering quiet support and reassurance. His presence was a pillar of strength for her, providing unwavering comfort and stability during a difficult time. Rose felt deeply grateful for his protective and supportive embrace.

"Thank you," she whispered through tearful breaths, her voice barely audible. "I didn't know if you'd come... but you did when I needed you the most." These words escaped her quivering lips as she looked up with gratitude, her eyes glistening with unshed tears.

Dean turned towards her, his eyes filled with warmth and understanding. His head tilted slightly as he nodded, showing his knowledge and support. "You're not alone, Rose. I'm here for you."

Taking a deep breath, Rose tried to calm herself down. "I've wasted so much time, Dean," she confessed, her voice cracking with emotion. "I let myself get stuck in a part of my life that I should've left behind long ago."

He gently squeezed her shoulder, his thumb brushing against her collarbone soothingly. "We all have chapters we wish we could rewrite or erase," he said softly. "But it's never too late to start a new one."

As they sat together, their shared silence spoke volumes - it was a testament to the depth of their connection, how they could communicate without words. Rose found comfort in Dean's steady embrace and leaned into him.

"Thank you once again, Dean," she said with renewed strength. You being here means everything to me. You've profoundly impacted my life and provided my heart with the needed support."

"Of course, Rose." He smiled warmly at her, his eyes crinkling at the corners. "What are friends for, right?"

At that moment, surrounded by flickering shadows and bathed in the soft golden light, it felt like time had slowed down. The weight of the past was heavy on their shoulders, but together, they found the strength to carry it.

"Right," Rose agreed with a barely audible whisper. "Friends."

The soft, muted light from the nearby lamp created an intimate atmosphere. Gentle shadows on the walls followed Rose, walking with a couple of tea cups.

Dean and Rose sat across from each other, a small table now between them, their hands clasped around steaming cups of tea.

With a trembling finger, Rose traced the delicate pattern on her teacup, lost in thought as she searched for the right words to express the turmoil in her heart.

"Dean," she began hesitantly, her gaze fixed on the swirling designs in her cup. "Lately, I've been thinking about courage. It's something we often don't realize we have until we need it."

She looked up at him, tears shimmering in her eyes. "Last night, when you were there for me... I saw what true courage looks like. And when I needed it the most, I found the strength to tap into it." Her voice wavered, but she continued, determined to convey just how much his support had meant to her.

"Thank you," she whispered, reaching out to take his hand. Their fingers entwined in a firm and reassuring grip.

Dean's gentle smile softened his features as he gave her hand a comforting squeeze. "That's what friends are for, Rose. To help each other face our fears and find courage we never knew we had."

Rose took a deep breath, her mind racing with thoughts that could no longer be bottled up. "You know," she confided in him, "I think most people don't break up because they've grown apart. They do it because they've become too comfortable in their relationships."

She paused for a moment before continuing with newfound determination. "Last night made me realize I no longer want to live comfortably. I want to live purposefully and on purpose." She met his gaze, her eyes filled with gratitude and determination. "And I couldn't have come to that realization without you being there for me when I needed you."

Dean's eyes never left her face as Rose poured her heart

out. He understood the struggle of breaking free from the familiar, even when it no longer served them.

"Rose," he promised, his voice thick with emotion, "I'll always be here for you. We'll face it together no matter what life throws our way."

A single tear slipped down Rose's cheek, but she smiled through it, her heart overflowing with love and appreciation for the man who had become her rock in such a short time. They sat there, hands still clasped, ready to take on whatever challenges the future held – with courage and purpose.

Like a ray of sunshine, a gentle smile illuminated Dean's face as he listened to Rose. Her words were like a healing balm for his weary soul, soothing his inner turmoil. As she spoke, he couldn't help but feel grateful for her presence in his life.

He traced delicate circles on the back of her hand with his fingers, savoring the warmth and comfort of her touch. "You know," he began softly, his voice filled with sincerity, "ever since I've known you, I've learned so much about good people and the inevitability of making mistakes."

Dean held her gaze, his eyes shining with admiration and understanding. "I truly believe that there are only a few perfect combinations of people who can bring out each other's full potential – combinations that only God knows." He paused, taking a deep breath before continuing. "Rose, you and Dominic must have crossed paths for a reason. Just like how I chose my band members for my reasons."

"However," he added firmly, determination lacing his words, "I believe that it was God who brought us together last night, and no weapon formed against us could ever prosper." He gently squeezed her hand. His conviction and belief radiated from him. "What God has joined together is significant, and I don't think anyone can break that bond."

Dean's eyes flickered with determination as he declared, "I plan to seek Pastor Dave's guidance in refining this message – to share it with others and help them understand the incredible power of divine guidance."

As Dean spoke, tears welled up in Rose's eyes. They spilled over and trailed down her cheeks like shimmering rivers, moved by the depth and intensity of his words. The atmosphere in the room seemed to shift, becoming almost ethereal as if time had paused to witness their connection.

"Dean," Rose whispered, her voice trembling with emotion, "I've always believed that God guides our steps, but moments like these make me feel it deep within my soul." She leaned in closer, her words barely a breath. "The importance of unwavering trust and faith in His guidance...

It's something I'll never take for granted again."

Their gazes remained locked, the unspoken understanding between them palpable. Dean and Rose had been profoundly changed by the events that had transpired, finding solace and strength in each other's unwavering support. Once battered and bruised, their hearts were now on a path of healing, guided ever so gently by a divine hand.

The soft hum of the air conditioner in the room provided a gentle background noise as Dean allowed his mind to wander back to that fateful day when their story began at an unassuming bus stop where everything seemed uncertain.

"Rose," he said softly, a hint of nostalgia in his voice, "I can't believe it was just yesterday when this whole thing started at the bus stop? I was feeling so lost, like I was drifting aimlessly through life. But then I heard this voice—" he paused, feeling a lump form in his throat—I believe it was God telling me that everything would be okay."

Rose's eyes lit up with wonder and emotion as she looked at him. "I remember," she replied, her voice barely above a whisper. "You walked up to me, and at that moment, you turned into a message for me by turning it into a beautiful song. It felt like... a lifeline."

Dean couldn't help but smile, grateful for the unexpected turn that had brought them together. "It felt like a lifeline to me, too, Rose. A lifeline that has kept us connected through all the ups and downs life has thrown our way."

Dean took a moment to survey their surroundings as they sat there, wrapped in the warm embrace of their shared memories. The room felt familiar and comforting, almost like a sanctuary for them.

"You know," he remarked, "this place looks wonderful. It feels like your own little haven."

A slight grimace crossed Rose's face as she followed Dean's gaze. "Maybe to you, Dean. But to me, it's filled with chaos and commotion." She shook her head, frustration evident in her tone. "Just today, another woman left her underwear in the bathroom. Can you believe that?"

Despite his best efforts, Dean couldn't hold back a chuckle at Rose's exasperation. He reached for her hand, giving it a reassuring squeeze. "Well, maybe your sanctuary isn't perfect right now. But as long as we have this, we can find solace and strength no matter what's happening around us."

At that moment, holding hands with Rose, the room seemed to take on a new meaning that transcended the physical space and encompassed the deep connection between two souls who had found each other against all odds.

And at that moment, any chaos and commotion faded

away, replaced by the quiet understanding that together, they could face anything life had in store.

The sun's warm rays cascaded through the sheer curtains, creating a new radiant glow that filled the room with tranquility. Dean and Rose moved to the couch, their fingers intertwined as they leaned into each other's embrace. Outside, the bustling world seemed to fade away, leaving only the two and the unbreakable bond that held them together.

"Rose," Dean's voice was soft but unwavering. "We can't let our past dictate our present or future. We must learn from it and move forward." He turned to her, his steady gaze conveying both strength and vulnerability. "You've been through so much, but please know I will always be here for you."

Tears welled in Rose's eyes as she looked at him with gratitude. "Thank you, Dean," she whispered, her voice trembling with emotion. "It's just...sometimes the negative thoughts are hard to shake."

"I understand," Dean said, reassuringly squeezing her hand. "But remember, negativity takes no effort. It's positivity that requires energy and determination." He smiled warmly at her. "And I have no doubt you possess an abundance of both."

Rose couldn't help but smile back, feeling some of her

worries melt away under his kind words. "You're wise beyond your years, Dean Winchester. Where did all this newfound philosophy come from?"

Dean laughed, his eyes sparkling mischievously. "Well, I wasn't always this philosophical," he admitted. "But being with you, spending time with you... it's changed me for the better. And now, I want to spread that positivity wherever I go."

Dean and Rose's words served as a healing balm for their hearts and souls as they continued talking. The power of their connection permeated through the room, filling it with a sense of peace and contentment. In that moment, as they sat together, gazing out at the world beyond, they were a testament to the transformative nature of love and friendship, offering hope to those who may be lost in their struggles.

"Dean," Rose whispered, her voice filled with gratitude. "Thank you for reminding me that there is always a light at the end of the tunnel, even when it feels like everything is falling apart."

Dean replied softly, his voice barely above a whisper, as he pulled Rose closer and wrapped his arm around her shoulders. The warmth of his touch was a reassurance, a physical manifestation of his words. 'Remember, we are stronger together, and nothing can tear us apart.'

Together, they faced whatever challenges lay ahead, their hearts full of hope and determination. As the golden sunlight continued to envelop them in its warm embrace, it was clear that their bond would only continue to grow stronger, fueled by love, faith, and an unshakable belief in the power of positivity.

The sun's light, a gentle caress, continued to dance through the sheer curtains, enveloping Rose and Dean in a warm, golden glow. Dean's hesitant voice, like a fragile thread, broke the quiet stillness between them, his words hanging heavy with unspoken emotions.

"You know, Rose," he began, cautiously choosing his words, "I don't think Dominic will be returning anytime soon. But I want you to know I'm here for you, no matter what happens."

A wave of gratitude washed over Rose, her heart touched by Dean's unwavering support. She met his gaze with a soft smile, her eyes reflecting the warmth and comfort she felt.

Dean glanced at his watch, furrowing his brow with concern. "I should start getting ready for my shift, but if you need me to stay longer, I can."

Rose's mind raced as she processed the implications of Dominic's absence and Dean's offer. Though her heart yearned for him to stay, she knew it was important for them to continue their daily lives.

"Go ahead, Dean. It would be best if you weren't late because of me," she said firmly, offering a reassuring smile. "Besides, I'll join you shortly after to help with the dinner rush."

"Only if you're sure," Dean hesitated for a moment, searching her face for any trace of uncertainty.

Rose nodded firmly, bolstered by their strong connection during their honest conversation. Deep down, she knew she could face whatever challenges ahead if Dean stood by her side.

The gears in Rose's mind whirred as she processed the implications of Dominic's absence and Dean's offer. While her heart longed for him to stay, she realized that both of them needed to continue with their daily lives.

"Go, Dean. It would be best if you weren't late because of me," she said, reassuringly smiling. "Besides, I'll join you shortly after to help with the dinner crowd."

"Only if you're sure," Dean hesitated momentarily, his eyes searching hers for any sign of uncertainty.

Rose nodded firmly, her resolve strengthened by the profound connection they'd forged during their heartfelt conversation. She knew she could face whatever lay ahead as long as Dean stood beside her.

"Alright then, I'll see you there," Dean said, returning

her smile. Standing up from the couch, he gently squeezed her hand, filling her with comfort and security.

As Dean walked towards the door, Rose's thoughts swirled with the possibilities of life beyond Dominic. For the first time in a long while, she felt excitement about the future, fueled by her newfound strength and the unwavering bond she shared with Dean.

"Dean?" she called softly as he reached for the door handle. He turned back to face her, his eyes filled with warmth and curiosity.

"Thank you," she whispered, her gratitude reverberating through every syllable, "for giving me the courage to embrace change."

"I can't wait to see you later," he said softly, his voice carrying the weight of their shared experiences. "I understand that this moment may be very emotional for you."

Rose nodded, her heart swelling with gratitude and love for the man who had become her rock amidst the chaos of her life. As Dean closed the door behind him, she leaned against it, taking a deep breath to steady herself.

Dean's smile deepened, his dimples carving crescents into his cheeks. "That's what friends are for, right?" With a final nod, he exited the apartment, leaving Rose to gather before facing the world beyond her front door.

As she also had to prepare to join Dean at the restaurant,

Rose couldn't help but marvel at the transformative power of friendship. In less than twenty-four hours, their bond had reinvigorated her spirit and illuminated a new path forward.

Amid all the uncertainty, knowing they were not alone was comforting. They had each other to rely on and face any life challenge that may come their way.

Chapter 15

The sun's bright rays illuminated the busy city streets, creating a warm and radiant atmosphere that enveloped Dean as he made his way to the restaurant. His mind was consumed with thoughts of Rose - her gentle demeanor, kind gaze, and how she had captured his heart in a way he never could have imagined.

A soft breeze brushed through his hair, but Dean hardly noticed as his mind recalled their conversations and shared moments. Each step felt lighter than the last, anticipation and joy bubbling within him at the mere thought of seeing her again.

Across town, Rose stood by her apartment window, gazing out at the city below. The sounds of traffic and people drifted up to her, but she was lost in her thoughts. Her neatly folded uniform lay on the bed behind her, forgotten for now.

She felt grateful for having met Dean, whose unwavering smile and passion for music had brought a new sense of joy into her life. With newfound hope, she whispered, "Everything is going to be okay."

At that very moment, Dean's phone vibrated in his pocket, jolting him back to reality. He pulled it out to see a call from a friend of the restaurant manager who had previously expressed interest in having him perform at an upcoming wedding.

"Hey, this is Dean," he answered eagerly, excited and curious.

"Dean! Hi!" The caller's voice was warm and friendly. "I'm so glad I caught you. We wanted to talk to you about performing at my friend's wedding. We've heard such wonderful things about your singing, and we'd love for you to be part of our special day."

"Really?" Dean's heart skipped a beat with possibility, his earlier thoughts of Rose mingling with dreams of sharing his music with others. "I'd be honored."

"Fantastic! I'll send you all the details later today. Thanks so much, Dean. We're looking forward to it."

"Thank you for thinking of me," he replied sincerely before ending the call. As he slipped his phone back into his pocket, he couldn't contain the smile that spread across his face. Excitement and anticipation bubbled within him as he thought about sharing this news with Rose at work. Their next meeting held even more promise now, and he couldn't wait to see where their relationship would lead.

The sun's gentle rays now danced like musical notes in his head down the street, casting a warm golden glow that enveloped Dean as he stood still, his heart swelling with anticipation.

His mind buzzed with excitement as he replayed the conversation, remembering how he had expressed his feelings of being lost and searching for something to reignite his passion. And now, that spark had finally come - an opportunity to perform at a wedding and share his music with others, igniting a fire within him.

"Dean, are you still on the line?" the voice on the other end asked, bringing him back to reality.

"Sorry," he chuckled nervously, "I'm just really excited. Thank you so much for giving me this chance."

"Of course! We were saddened to hear about your band

breaking up. But we've heard so much about your heartfelt singing; we truly believe that's what our special day needs. Your talent deserves to be shared with the world."

Those words resonated deeply within Dean, fueling his desire to make the most of this opportunity. His fingers tapped rhythmically against his thigh as he imagined himself standing before a crowd, pouring his soul into each note he sang.

"Thank you from the bottom of my heart," he replied sincerely, his voice thick with gratitude. "I promise I'll give it my all and make your wedding an unforgettable experience."

"Amazing!" the caller responded enthusiastically. "We'll email you all the details later today. And again, thank you, Dean. We can't wait to have you be part of our celebration."

"Neither can I," Dean said with a smile spreading across his face. With one final word of thanks, he hung up the phone, his heart racing excitedly.

Dean was overcome with a newfound sense of purpose as the call ended. This was more than just a performance—it was an opportunity to prove to himself and the world that he could achieve his dreams. He looked down at his phone, the screen now dark, and thought of Rose.

She had become a beacon of hope for him, her unwavering belief in his talents giving him the strength to believe in himself. He longed to tell her about this chance and share his excitement, knowing she would be just as thrilled.

As Dean began returning to the restaurant where they both worked, his steps felt lighter, more purposeful. His mind was filled with images of the upcoming performance, each note ringing out like a promise to himself and Rose.

He couldn't wait to see her again, to share this news with her, and to embark on this new chapter of their lives together, hand in hand. The bustling streets seemed to fade away as Dean's thoughts consumed the potential and possibilities of what would come.

Dean stepped into the small store, its fluorescent lights flickering above him like a night beacon. He took a deep breath as he remembered the tense events from the previous night, his heart still fluttering from the adrenaline rush.

But amidst the lingering fear and anxiety, a new sense of optimism bloomed within him. Walking to the counter, he noticed the same cashier who had been there during the robbery. The young man's eyes widened in recognition as he gave Dean a weak smile, his face still bearing traces of the trauma they had both experienced.

"Hey, it's you again," the cashier said, quivering slightly.

"Thanks for what you did last night. You helped keep everyone safe."

Dean returned the smile, his eyes filled with warmth and understanding for this brave young man. "No problem, just glad I could help. How are you holding up?"

"Better now, thanks to you," the cashier replied, studying Dean more closely with curiosity sparkling in his eyes. "Are you sure you're not famous or something? There's just something about you I can't put my finger on."

Dean chuckled and shook his head. "I'm sure. But I did just get offered a gig to perform at a wedding. It's not fame, but it's a start."

His excitement was palpable as he shared the news, his hands gesturing animatedly while his words flowed with passion and determination. Each syllable carried the weight of his dreams, nurtured since childhood, and the opportunity that now lay before him. The fire in his eyes burned bright, fueled by the desire to make every moment count and turn his dreams into reality.

"Wow, congratulations!" the cashier exclaimed, genuinely happy for him. "You must be thrilled. It's amazing how life can change in an instant, huh?"

"Definitely," Dean agreed with a smile, thinking of Rose and the difference she had made in his life. With her by his side, anything seemed possible.

In the meantime, Rose strolled down a quiet street, her fingers tightly clutching the bag of carefully selected gifts. Her face displayed an unmistakable sense of doubt, revealing her inner conflicts as she neared a familiar cardboard box hidden in the shadows.

The sound of her footsteps pierced the quietness of the day until she finally arrived at her destination. With a deep breath to calm her nerves, she hesitantly tapped on the box, feeling her heart race in anticipation.

"Who's there?" came the voice from within the box, its rough timbre softened by kindness and gratitude.

"It's me, Rose," she replied, trying to sound more confident than she felt.

"Ah, Miss Rose," Tim said warmly. "How are you doing today?"

"Doing fine, thank you," she answered with a small smile playing on her lips. "And how about you, Tim? How are you doing?"

"Same as always, just taking life one day at a time," he replied, his voice strong despite his circumstances.

Taking courage from his resilience and unwavering spirit, Rose held out the bag of gifts. "I brought you something. I thought these might help brighten your day."

"Thank you," Tim whispered, touched by her kindness and thoughtfulness. "You didn't have to do this, but it means the world to me."

As Rose carefully placed the bag of gifts into Tim's quivering hands, she couldn't help but feel a surge of emotions welling up inside her. The weight of her words hung heavily in the air as she spoke with a hint of vulnerability, "I thought these things would look so lovely on you," her voice trembling with emotion.

"Thank you," Tim managed to choke out, tears glittering as he looked down at the neatly wrapped presents. His hands shook slightly as he held onto them. "I can't remember the last time someone bought me a gift," he confessed, his voice thick with emotion. "And one that was gift-wrapped at that."

Rose's heart felt heavy with empathy for him. She remembered the profound wisdom and kindness he had shared with her and Dean just the night before, how his words had resonated deep within her soul. "Tim, what you gave us last night was a precious gift," she told him earnestly. "These gifts are just a small token of our appreciation for you."

Their eyes locked in a moment of understanding, and Rose saw something shift within Tim - disbelief giving way to a glimmer of hope. Overcome with emotion, he retreated into the box to open the gifts, but not before offering her a folding chair. "Please, have a seat while I look at this," he said, his voice barely above a whisper.

"Thank you, Tim," Rose replied gratefully, settling onto the chair. As she watched him disappear into the box, she couldn't help but reflect on the power of human connection and reaching out to someone in need. She also pondered on the beauty of giving without expecting anything in return.

Soft sunlight seeped through the crevices of Tim's flimsy cardboard dwelling, illuminating a stack of gift boxes in front of him. The warm rays brought a sense of optimism and compassion as he gingerly peeled back the wrapping on the first present. Meanwhile, outside on a folding chair, Rose anxiously waited for any movement as she heard the faint crinkle of paper being opened.

Tim exclaimed in awe as he revealed a crisp, dark green button-up shirt from the box, its fabric catching the sunlight like a precious gemstone. His fingers traced the intricate stitching, marveling at the softness of the material. Closing his eyes momentarily, he breathed in new clothes, a fragrance that carried memories of better days.

Lost in her thoughts, Rose allowed herself to meditate on her life—her struggles and the unexpected friendship she had formed with Dean. Through their journey together and meeting Tim, she truly understood the importance of giving and receiving love.

As time passed, Rose's excitement and anticipation grew. She couldn't wait to see Tim's reaction to the gifts, hoping they would bring him a small measure of joy on his arduous journey.

Finally, Tim emerged from the box with pure gratitude and disbelief. "You didn't have to do this for me," he said, his voice trembling with emotion. "But I can't thank you enough, Rose."

"Your words last night were a gift to us, too, Tim," she responded softly, tears welling up in her eyes. "We're all taking care of each other on this journey, aren't we?" Her heart felt full as she gazed at Tim's transformed expression, grateful for the unexpected bond they had formed through their simple acts of giving and receiving.

Overwhelmed with emotion, Tim with tears glistening in his eyes. "Rose... I don't even know what to say," he choked out. "This is too much."

"Please don't worry about it, Tim," Rose reassured him, her eyes filling with tears as she saw his reaction. "We wanted to do this for you. You deserve to feel good about yourself, and if these clothes can help, then we're happy."

Through tear-filled eyes, Tim replied, "Nobody has ever done anything like this for me, Rose. I didn't think people still cared."

"Of course, we care," Rose insisted, wiping away a tear.

"Dean and I may have only known you briefly, but you've already touched our hearts. We want to help you in any way we can."

Filled with gratitude, Tim said softly, "Your kindness means more to me than I could ever say. I'll cherish these gifts for their material value and as a reminder that there are still good people who genuinely care."

With a warm smile, Rose replied, "Then our mission is accomplished. But don't forget Tim; you have a gift too. Your wisdom and spirit have made a difference in Dean's and my life. You must remember there's always hope, no matter how dark things seem."

As Rose spoke those heartfelt words, she felt warmth and connection with Tim, knowing they had formed a bond beyond mere circumstance. This moment would be etched in her memory as a testament to the power of compassion and friendship.

"Thank you, Rose," Tim whispered, his voice heavy with unshed tears. "I'll never forget what you and Dean have done for me."

"And we will never forget you, Tim," Rose replied, gently squeezing his hand. "We're all in this together, and we'll continue walking each other home."

"Think of these clothes as breadcrumbs, Tim," Rose spoke softly but with conviction. "They're here to remind you that the person you once were is still inside you. You must return to him, one step at a time."

Tim nodded slowly, tears welling as he clutched the clothes tightly. "You're right, Rose. It's been so long since I've felt this kind of hope." "We all need someone to believe in us, Tim," Rose replied, her voice trembling with emotion. "And we believe in you. You have so much wisdom and strength within you. Please never forget that."

As they sat together, bathed in the sun's warm glow, Rose couldn't help but feel a deep connection with Tim. By reaching out to him, she had helped him rediscover a part of himself and found a new sense of purpose within her heart. She knew this experience would remind her of the transformative power of kindness and compassion.

"Thank you, Rose," Tim whispered, his voice thick with gratitude. "I won't forget what you've done for me – what you both have done."

"Neither will we, Tim," Rose responded, reassuringly squeezing his hand. "We're all on this journey together, and we'll continue to support each other every step of the way."

The restaurant was also bathed in the warm, golden light of the late afternoon sun, creating a welcoming and cozy ambiance. Dean moved remarkably gracefully through the labyrinth of bustling tables, deftly balancing a heavy tray piled high with dirty dishes on his muscular arm.

He skillfully maneuvered through the crowded space with each deliberate step, ensuring no single drop was spilled or dish dropped. Amidst the lively conversations of the restaurant and the gentle clinking of silverware and glasses, a harmonious symphony of sounds filled the air, adding to the vibrant energy of the restaurant.

Amidst this organized chaos, Dean remained calm and composed, his focus unwavering as he went to a nearby counter to set down the tray. Suddenly, a familiar voice called out to him, cutting through the noise like a ray of sunshine.

"Hey, Dean!" Rose greeted him with a radiant smile as she entered the restaurant. Her eyes immediately found him among the sea of people, drawing him in with her infectious energy. With confident steps, she made her way over to him, her long, flowing hostess dress swaying gently with each movement as the soft light from the chande-liers above caught the sparkle in her eyes. The sound of her heels clicking against the floor echoed through the bustling restaurant, and the sweet scent of her perfume lingered in the air as she approached him with a warm and welcoming presence.

"Hey there, Rose!" Dean's face lit up with a warm smile at the sight of her, his heart fluttering slightly at her mere presence. "How was your morning?"

"It was great," Rose replied enthusiastically, hinting at some newfound sense of purpose. "I had an extraordinary chat with Tim earlier."

Dean's concern for their homeless friend was immediately piqued. "How's he doing?"

"Better, I think," Rose shared, her expression softening at the memory. "I gave him some gifts from us, and we had a heart-to-heart. It was extraordinary."

A warmth spread through Dean's chest at Rose and Tim sharing a meaningful moment. "That's amazing, Rose. You have such a big heart."

Rose flashed him a playful grin before getting straight to the point. "Speaking of hearts... you have some exciting news, too, don't you?"

Dean couldn't contain his excitement any longer as he recalled the phone call he had received earlier that day. "Yes! I got offered a gig to perform at a wedding! It's an incredible opportunity and could help boost my music career."

"Dean, that's fantastic!" Rose beamed with pride. "Tell me more – where is it? When?"

"It's in two weeks at The Willow Grove, this beautiful venue just outside of town," Dean gushed, his enthusiasm contagious. "They heard about my heartfelt singing and think I'm perfect for their big day."

"This is amazing, Dean! You deserve this chance, and I know you'll make a great impression on everyone there," Rose encouraged, her unwavering faith in him shining through.

"Thank you, Rose," Dean murmured with gratitude. "Your support means everything to me. I couldn't have done any of this without you."

Dean and Rose shared a connection that transcended words as the lively buzz of the restaurant continued around them. Amid chaos and noise, they found solace in one another, their hearts bound by a strong bond that grew stronger each day.

The warm sunlight poured through the restaurant's large windows, creating a dotted pattern on the floor as it filtered through the swaying branches of nearby trees. Rose couldn't help but be mesmerized by Dean's intense gaze, which seemed to pierce through her soul. For a moment, it was as if they were the only two people in the world, connected by an invisible thread that pulsed with their shared emotions.

"Meeting you was like flipping a switch inside of me," Dean confessed softly, his voice filled with raw emotion. The vulnerability in his eyes spoke volumes about the depth of his feelings for her.

Blushing delicately, Rose smiled in response, her voice barely audible. "My light was off until you came along," she replied, grateful for his presence and impact on her life.

The clinking of silverware and glasses reminded them of the bustling atmosphere, returning them to reality. Another hostess approached them apologetically: "Rose, I'm sorry to interrupt, but we need you to start your shift early. We're getting slammed."

"Of course!" Rose replied cheerfully, determined not to let this plan change affect her mood. She rose gracefully, turned, and followed the hostess toward the busy dining area, leaving Dean to watch her with a mix of pride and affection.

As service continued, Dean and Rose worked diligently to provide exceptional service to every patron who walked through their doors. Despite the chaos and flurry of activity, they found comfort knowing they worked together in this fast-paced environment.

While clearing tables and refilling drinks, Dean couldn't resist stealing glances at Rose, marveling at how effortlessly she managed the demands of their job with a warm smile and compassionate demeanor. He couldn't help but feel his heart swell with love and admiration for her.

In rare moments of respite, when their eyes met from across the room, Dean and Rose exchanged knowing smiles, communicating their shared connection amidst the chaos. Their silent glances spoke of unspoken promises and dreams for the future, offering a calming oasis amidst the hectic world around them.

Amidst the cacophony of voices, laughter, and clanking dishes, Dean and Rose found solace in the deep, warm emotions they shared. Though their hands were busy with work, their hearts remained intertwined, drawing strength and inspiration from one another as they navigated life's challenges together.

The sunlight streaming through the windows of the bustling restaurant seemed to dance on Rose's skin as she eagerly awaited Pastor Dave's arrival. Her eyes sparkled with anticipation as she saw him entering, his warm presence radiating kindness and wisdom as he made his way through the crowd.

He was accompanied by eight people who seemed to exude a sense of serenity in his presence. They followed him with reverence as he navigated the busy eatery with an air of quiet grace.

Rose couldn't contain her excitement as she approached the group, her smile bright and genuine. "Welcome to our restaurant, Pastor Dave!" she exclaimed. "Please allow me to assist you with your seating arrangements."

Pastor Dave returned her smile, his eyes crinkling at

the corners in genuine warmth. "Thank you, Rose. I'm delighted to be here," he replied. "I wanted to be the first to visit and see you and Dean." His gaze swept across the room, eventually landing on Dean – busy attending to other customers – who acknowledged their exchange with a friendly wave from a distance.

A warm sensation filled Rose's chest as she led the group to a large table near the center of the dining area. As she pulled out chairs for each guest, she couldn't help but reflect on Pastor Dave's impact on her and Dean's lives. At this moment, she only strengthened her resolve to change her life positively.

"We're happy to have you here, Pastor Dave," Rose said, her voice soft yet steady. "The restaurant thanks you, and so do Dean and I. We plan on visiting your church very soon, this time during the daytime."

"Ah, that would be wonderful," Pastor Dave responded, his tone warm and inviting. "Our doors are always open to both of you because our community welcomes all with open arms," he added, his sincerity palpable. Pastor Dave's kind, gentle eyes met Rose's, their warmth radiating through the bustling restaurant. The sound of clinking dishes and customers' chatter faded as he spoke.

The words struck a chord in Rose's heart, and she turned to Dean, who was diligently wiping down a nearby table. Their eyes met, mirroring the hope and determination sparked within her.

"Thank you, Pastor Dave," she said gratefully. "We will make sure to attend."

As Rose finished assisting the group, she took a moment to steal another glance at Dean, who seemed to balance a tray of dishes while effortlessly navigating between tables. She marveled at how they found comfort and solace in one another's presence, even amidst the chaos and noise.

With a sense of accomplishment and satisfaction, Rose thought, "Alright, everyone is settled. Now it's time to get back to work."

Dean walked over, sensing the gravity of the moment. As he reached Rose's side, he took her hand in his, their fingers intertwining like two souls bound by fate. At that moment, it felt like they were making a solemn vow to attend church and embrace the path ahead of them.

"Are you ready for this?" Dean asked softly, his voice barely audible above the restaurant's noise.

Rose nodded, feeling a surge of determination coursing through her veins. "Yes, I am."

Their faces were solemn as they stood hand-in-hand, symbolizing their commitment to taking control of their lives and starting anew.

"Here's to us," Dean whispered, his gaze locked with

Rose's.

"Here's to a fresh start," she agreed wholeheartedly.

Rose couldn't help but marvel at how far they had come since their first encounter as they released each other's hands and returned to their duties. From strangers to friends, confidants, and now something more profound – their bond had blossomed into an unbreakable connection that promised to guide them through life's trials and tribulations.

"See you later, Pastor Dave!" Rose called out cheerfully as they went back to work.

"Take care, my dear," Pastor Dave replied, his eyes gleaming with pride and hope for the young couple before him.

As they worked together in harmony, Rose's mind was filled with thoughts of the future—a life built on faith, love, and the unwavering support of their community.

As she watched Dean gracefully maneuver through the busy restaurant, she knew deep in her heart that together, they could conquer anything.

Amidst the clanging of cutlery and bursts of laughter from patrons, Dean couldn't help but steal glances at Rose as she expertly seated a family of four with grace and efficiency. Their eyes would meet briefly, her shy smile tugging at his heartstrings every time.

"Hey, Dean?" Her voice barely rose above the noisy chatter of the restaurant, but to him, it was like a sweet melody cutting through the chaos. "Do you think we could...spend our break together?"

His heart leaped with excitement and anticipation when she extended her invitation, causing him to forget his responsibilities as he nodded eagerly momentarily. "Without a doubt! I would be delighted to join you, Rose."

With a graceful and fluid movement, she closed the distance between them, her steps almost dancing as she moved. Gently, she pressed her lips to his flushed cheek, the warmth of her touch lingering like a sweet, fleeting caress. As she turned away to resume her tasks, Dean felt as if he was suspended in mid-air, enveloped in a moment of serenity amid the bustling chaos of the restaurant.

As the lunch break approached, whispers and excited chatter spread among their co-workers. Dean and Rose's budding romance had captured the hearts of their co-workers, and the prospect of them sharing a meal filled the atmosphere with palpable anticipation. Sensing the buzz, the manager proposed a plan to make the occasion even more special.

"Why not have their lunch during our break between lunch and dinner service?" he proposed to the rest of the staff. "We can all pitch in to make it special for them."

The team erupted in cheers, eager to play a part in creating a memorable moment for their friends.

Now aware of the plans, Dean couldn't help feeling nervous and excited. He knew this lunch had a deeper meaning than just food shared between friends; it symbolized their growing connection and a testament to their love blossoming.

Dean watched as their break finally arrived, and their co-workers hurriedly transformed a restaurant corner into an intimate dining space. A small, beautifully set table stood before them, adorned with a vibrant bouquet and two flickering candles in the dim lighting. The air was buzzing with anticipation.

"Wow," Rose murmured in awe as she joined Dean at the table. "This is incredible."

He couldn't help but smile, his eyes filled with affection. "It's all thanks to our amazing team," he replied, reaching for her hand across the table. "But really, I think it's perfect...because it's with you."

As they shared their meal and conversation flowed effortlessly between them, the outside world seemed to fade away until all that remained were two souls connected by love and hope for the future. As the last morsels of food disappeared from their plates, Dean knew that this simple lunch had become a moment he would treasure forever.

Chapter 16

The soft, golden glow of candles danced across the elegantly set table, casting a warm and intimate light over Dean and Rose. The low hum of conversations and clinking glasses from their restaurant co-workers faded into the background, leaving them wrapped in their private world.

Dean's eyes sparkled with adoration as they sat facing each other. His smile spread wide, and he listened intently to every word from Rose's lips. His fingers lightly tapped on the crisp white tablecloth, a subtle habit born from years of also playing the piano—a small, comforting reminder of his love for music.

"Dean, do you remember when I was making tea, I heard you keep singing to yourself?" Rose asked with a slight pink flush, coloring her cheeks at the memory.

Dean chuckled softly, his hand rubbing the back of his neck in embarrassment. "Ah yes, I didn't. You were listening."

"Well, I'm glad I was," Rose said softly, her eyes shining sincerely. "Your voice is like the honey I put in the tea, and it made me feel like your song says everything was going to be ok."

A warmth spread through Dean's chest at her words, and a genuine smile graced his lips. "Thank you, Rose. That means more to me than you know."

As they continued to talk and share stories, the waitstaff glided over to their table, gracefully balancing trays of steaming dishes. The smell of savory herbs and spices filled the air as the plates were laid before them.

Dean and Rose, who were used to ordering simple meals on their breaks, were surprised when the waitstaff presented them with extravagant dishes fit for a fine dining experience. The aromas and presentation made this moment feel like an actual date rather than just a break from work. They could practically taste the effort and care put into each dish by the talented chefs.

"Wow, this looks amazing," Rose marveled at the exquisite presentation of her dish, taking in the tantalizing aroma that wafted through the air.

"I know, right?" Dean agreed, admiring the colorful arrangement of his meal. "We should've been more adventurous instead of eating sandwiches during our breaks."

They both dug into their food with relish, appreciating every bite. Their conversation flowed naturally and effortlessly as if they had known each other for years rather than twenty-four hours. They delved into various topics, from their hopes and dreams to the unique quirks that made them who they were.

"Rose, I've been meaning to ask you," Dean said, pausing with his fork mid-air. "What inspired you to work at the restaurant?"

She hesitated momentarily, taking a small sip of her wine as she gathered her thoughts. "I guess I needed a change of scenery – a fresh start. And I thought working here might help me find my footing again."

Dean nodded in understanding. His reasons for taking the job were not too different from hers. "Sometimes, new beginnings can be scary, but they can also bring exciting opportunities, right?"

"Definitely," Rose agreed, smiling shyly across the table. "Sometimes, they lead you to incredible people and experiences you never imagined."

As their plates gradually emptied and the evening wore on, the possibility of a future together seemed to fill the space between them. It was a future brimming with joy, warmth, support, and understanding – a future where perhaps they could both finally discover their true selves. But for now, they savored the present moment, two souls brought together by chance and bound by the enchantment of connection.

A delicate glow radiated from the flickering candlelight, casting a soft and romantic aura over Rose's features. The warm light reflected in her eyes, mirroring the tiny flame's gentle flickers. As she spoke to Dean, their hands occasionally brushed against each other like leaves rustling in a serene breeze, adding an intimate touch to their conversation.

"Dean, you know what I realized?" Rose's voice was barely above a whisper.

"What is it?" Dean leaned closer, his heart racing with anticipation.

"Being here with you... it feels like we've found something missing from our lives for so long."

He nodded, feeling a mix of nerves and excitement. "I

feel the same way, Rose. It's incredible how much has changed since we met."

Dean couldn't help but marvel at their undeniable connection as they continued to talk. It was as if fate had brought them together, two lost souls finding comfort in one another amidst the chaos of life.

"Can I try some of your food, Dean?" Rose asked suddenly, her eyes sparkling with curiosity.

"Of course!" He eagerly pushed his plate towards her, only for her to slide it back with a playful grin.

"You can feed me, Dean," she said softly, her cheeks glowing with a rosy hue.

Surprised yet delighted by her request, Dean placed his silverware on his plate as he reached for the fork she offered him. Before preparing a bite for her, he looked up at the sky and whispered a silent thank you to whoever brought Rose into his life.

He carefully speared a piece of food with a smile and held it to her. As she closed her lips around the fork, their eyes locked, and everything else seemed to fade away. In that moment, all that mattered was their undeniable bond and the endless possibilities ahead.

"Delicious," Rose murmured, still gazing into Dean's eyes. "But not as amazing as these twenty-four hours have been."

"Agreed," Dean replied softly, his heart swelling with emotion. "Here's to many more nights like this, Rose."

"Cheers," she whispered back, raising her glass to toast their newfound love and the endless possibilities before them.

The clinking of glasses and the faint sound of music filled the air, creating the perfect ambiance for this magical evening. As they continued to bask in each other's company, it was clear that this was only the beginning of their unforgettable journey together.

The soft, flickering glow of candlelight danced across the table, illuminating Rose's face with a warm, golden hue. Her eyes sparkled as she looked at Dean, her expression filled with love and affection. The air was filled with the gentle hum of their conversation, like a babbling brook flowing through a peaceful forest.

The outside world faded away as they shared stories and dreams that had long been hidden within their souls. It was just the two of them, wrapped in a cocoon of newfound love. But their intimate moment was interrupted by a hesitant but determined voice.

"Excuse me," the manager interjected apologetically. "I'm sorry to interrupt, but someone at the door asks to see you both."

Dean furrowed his brow in confusion while Rose's eyes

shimmered with an unspoken secret. She smiled warmly at the manager and said, "Please, let them in."

With a nod, the manager left to retrieve the visitor. And when they arrived at their table, it was as if time stood still.

Dean's mouth fell open in shock, his jaw practically hitting the ground. A rush of emotion filled Rose's eyes, tears of pure joy spilling over and tracing down her cheeks. Before them stood Tim, a man wholly transformed from the ragged figure they once knew.

His appearance was immaculate, every hair neatly groomed and every crease in his clothing expertly pressed. The air around him seemed to radiate with newfound confidence and dignity, a far cry from the broken and defeated man he used to be. It was as if he had emerged from a cocoon, fully embracing his new self with grace and poise.

"Tim!" Dean exclaimed, his heart bursting with happiness. "You look incredible! It's like a miracle!"

"It truly is," Tim replied with unwavering strength. "But I couldn't have done it without your help. You and Rose gave me hope when I needed it most."

Rose spoke softly, "Actually, we gave you something earlier today that may have played a part in this transformation." She smiled knowingly at Tim, who nodded gratefully.

"I owe so much to you both," he admitted with tears in his eyes. "I couldn't have found my way back to the old Tim without your unwavering support and kindness."

Tears began to spill from Rose's eyes as she reached to touch Tim's arm, her heart overflowing with love and gratitude. Dean exchanged a meaningful glance with the restaurant manager, who quickly understood the unspoken request. The manager approached Tim with an inviting smile.

"Please join us, Mr. Tim," he said graciously. We'd be honored to have you at our table tonight, and your meal is on the house."

Tim hesitated momentarily, his face a mixture of surprise and gratitude, before accepting the invitation with a heartfelt smile. He sat beside Dean, and the three friends marveled at the journey that had brought them together – from strangers to kindred spirits, bound by the threads of fate and the power of love.

Each bite of the meal was a burst of flavor as Tim sat with his loved ones, relishing every moment. The atmosphere was filled with joy and merriment, their laughter blending like a symphony. As he ate, memories flashed through his mind - days spent sleeping in a flimsy cardboard box, surviving on nothing but beans.

And now, here he was at this table, surrounded by

warmth and friendship, realizing just how far he had come. A journey of perseverance and determination led him to this moment of contentment and gratitude.

With a grateful smile, he raised his glass in a toast to their incredible journey – from strangers to kindred spirits, bound by fate and the power of love. "To new beginnings," he whispered, his heart full of gratitude for the beautiful tapestry of life that had brought them together.

Dean, Rose, and Tim linger at the table, savoring the warmth of their newfound camaraderie as the final crumbs of their delectable meal disappear from their plates. The gentle clink of silverware against porcelain gives way to a tranquil silence, punctuated only by the soft murmur of conversations from nearby tables.

"Guys," Dean began, his voice tinged with excitement, "I just remembered something I wanted to share with you both. I've been offered a chance to showcase my music at a wedding next week."

"Really?" Tim's eyes flickered joyfully, reflecting his deep-rooted happiness for his friend. "That's incredible, Dean!"

"Thank you," Dean replied humbly, his hand rubbing nervously at the back of his neck. "We never really talked about my music before, but it's always been my dream to make a living doing what I love."

Tim nodded thoughtfully, his gaze contemplative. "I can see why your soulful nature would translate beautifully into a song. I can't wait to hear you perform."

Rose chimed in, her eyes sparkling with pride as she gazed affectionately at Dean. "I do not doubt that your performance will be breathtaking. Your passion for music is contagious, and I know it will touch everyone who enjoys hearing it."

"Thanks, Rose," Dean replied bashfully, a faint blush dusting his cheeks under her praise.

The conversation then turned to Tim, who eagerly shared his progress since their last night's heartfelt discussion. "Talking with you motivated me to make positive changes in my life. Today, I went to the local shelter to get cleaned up. And I even signed up to pursue my education. It's time for me to start moving forward, don't you think?"

Dean and Rose exchanged proud glances before rising from their seats and giving Tim a heartfelt standing ovation, their hands clapping resoundingly to celebrate his efforts. "We're so proud of you, Tim!" Rose exclaimed, her face glowing.

"Thank you both," Tim replied, his voice thick with emotion. "Your support means everything to me. It's reminded me that I am more than my circumstances and that I have the potential to become who I once was."

As the trio basked in the radiance of their shared triumphs, they knew that fate had brought them together for a reason. Bound by love, empathy, and a common desire to better themselves, they faced the future with renewed hope and determination, ready to embrace whatever adventures life had in store for them.

Rose's gaze shifted between Dean and Tim, her cerulean eyes shimmering with unshed tears as she searched for the right words to express her gratitude. The warm glow of candlelight danced across their faces, giving them an ethereal quality and highlighting their shared deep connection.

Rose's voice was a soothing melody that seemed to dance on the breeze as she spoke. Every word she uttered held weight and meaning; it was as if each syllable was carefully chosen to convey the depth of her emotions. "Dean," she began, her eyes conveying a heartfelt sincerity. "You have shown me the true meaning of a home - it's more than just a physical space. It's a sanctuary where I can be myself and pursue my dreams again."

Her breath caught in her throat as she poured out her gratitude. "You have reignited my passion for art and reminded me of the beauty in life; I will always be grateful for that." The sincerity in her words hung in the air, lingering like a sweet fragrance long after they were spoken.

A playful smile tugged at the corners of her lips, revealing a dimple on one cheek as she nudged Dean gently with her elbow. Her eyes brimmed with love and fondness, sparkling in the sunlight that filtered through the window. "Now, I have a little question for you," she said teasingly.

With trembling hands, she reached into her purse and retrieved a set of keys, holding them out to him like a precious treasure. The cool metal glinted in the light, reflecting the excitement and nervousness in her expression. "Would you like to make this place our home? Move in with me?" Every word was spoken earnestly as if these simple keys held the key to their future together.

Dean's emerald green eyes widened in disbelief and uncertainty as he stared at the keys in his hand. Sensing the moment's significance, the restaurant co-workers burst into encouraging cheers and applause. After what felt like an eternity, Dean finally took the keys from Rose's outstretched hand and asked hesitantly, "Are you sure?"

She nodded emphatically, tears now spilling freely down her cheeks as she pulled him into a warm embrace. They both knew that this was just the beginning of something extraordinary.

With their living arrangements with Dean now settled, Rose turned her attention to Tim, who had watched their exchange with awe and admiration. His eyes were wide and shining, like a child on Christmas morning. "Tim," she said softly, placing a gentle hand on his shoulder, "you have been through so much, and I can't bear the thought of you returning to that cold, damp cardboard box.

So, I would like to offer you a place to stay with us until." Her voice was warm and full of genuine concern, matching the kind smile on her face. The room suddenly felt brighter, as if Rose's kindness had brought sunlight into the dim room. Tim's heart swelled with gratitude, and he couldn't hold back tears of relief and joy.

The weight of her words hit Tim like a tidal wave, and his head dropped as tears streamed down his face. Dean, concerned, asked if Tim would accept their offer. Through sobs, Tim nodded vigorously, overwhelmed by their kindness and generosity.

A week later, the three friends stood together at the wedding reception - a united front against the world. Dean nervously fiddled with his guitar pick as he prepared to take the stage while Rose offered encouragement and reassurance.

"Look at Tim," she said proudly, gesturing towards the dance floor where their friend was gracefully twirling around with an attractive lady, laughing and enjoying the night. "He has come so far, and it's all thanks to you."

Dean couldn't help but beam with happiness at the sight of Tim thriving. He felt a renewed sense of confidence wash over him as he turned back to Rose. "With you in the audience," he said, placing a hand over his heart, "I know I can give it my all tonight." He took a deep breath and continued, "D.J.'s got most of the music covered, so I need to focus on a few songs. And having you there for me... that's all I need."

As Dean stepped onto the stage, his heart filled with love and determination, he knew they had the power to overcome any obstacle life threw their way together. With each strum of his guitar and every note that escaped his lips, he poured his soul into the performance - each one a testament to the unbreakable bonds of friendship and love that had brought them together.

The grand reception hall fell silent as Dean gracefully took the stage, his fingers gliding over the strings of his acoustic guitar with expert precision. His voice was a haunting melody, powerful and soothing at once. As he sang a soulful ballad dedicated to Rose, the emotion in every word enveloped the room.

> "Your money is down, don't get down,
> I'm coming around, I can't let you down,
> Now take that frown and spin it around,
> Don't you worry about a thang babe,
> I can't let you have to want, lady,
> It's ok, 'cause I'm here to take away the strain."

Like precious jewels, tears glistened in Rose's eyes as she listened with rapt attention. Her heart swelled with pride and love for the man who had transformed her life. She couldn't resist glancing at Tim, standing nearby with his dance partner, equally captivated by Dean's performance.

The raw emotion emanating from Dean's every movement held the entire room in its thrall, a symphony of joy and sorrow woven together by his skilled hands and passionate spirit. Rose could feel her soul being lifted and carried away on the waves of music, lost in the moment with those she loved most.

As the last note faded into silence, a brief moment of stillness descended upon the room as if time had stopped to honor Dean and Rose's profound connection. The bride then approached Rose with a bouquet of delicate white flowers, her eyes shimmering with unshed tears.

"Nobody deserves this more than you," she whispered to Rose, her voice thick with emotion. "Thank you for allowing us to witness such a beautiful moment on our special day."

Rose accepted the bouquet gratefully, her cheeks flushed with gratitude and happiness. Tim could not contain his admiration as he approached Dean and Rose, his eyes shining.

"The way you played just now was incredible," he said

earnestly, clapping Dean on the back. "It's all because of the love you two share."

"Thank you, Tim," Dean replied humbly, his gaze never leaving Rose's face. "She makes everything easy for me."

Tim grinned and motioned towards his friend across the room, with whom he had been dancing all night. "Let me make things easier for you, too," he declared adamantly. "You've both been such good friends to me, and I want to return the favor."

Dean and Rose exchanged a knowing smile as they acknowledged Tim's dance partner. They witnessed their blossoming friendship throughout the evening, filled with laughter and joy.

"Thank you, Tim," Rose said sincerely. "We're overjoyed to see you enjoying yourself and finding happiness too."

As the night wore on, the three friends celebrated their triumphs and cherished the bonds they had formed, each step forward illuminated by the love and support they shared. The music continued to play, but the melody of their hearts resonated throughout the room, creating a harmonious symphony of friendship, love, and happiness.

Tim's eyes softened as he looked at his newfound friend across the opulent reception hall. She was swaying to the music, her face glowing with pure happiness, embraced by the warm light that seemed to radiate from within her.

Tim leaned closer to Dean and Rose, his voice tinged with vulnerability.

As Tim spoke, his voice was filled with pride and gratitude, his eyes meeting each of theirs with camaraderie. "Guys, I have something important to share with you," he announced. "She's a veteran like me."

The room fell silent as Tim's words hung in the air, heavy with unspoken memories and shared experiences. Dean's expression turned somber as he nodded in understanding, his mind drifting to thoughts of his parents, who had made the ultimate sacrifice while serving.

"Thank you for everything you've done, Tim," he said sincerely. "And thank you for sharing this with us." As his words echoed through the room, a sense of reverence and respect settled over the group as they recognized the weight of Tim's service and sacrifice.

Rose joined in, her tender eyes shining with admiration. "Yes, thank you for your service and for trusting us with this part of your story."

A soft smile tugged at the corners of Tim's mouth as he continued, "She's been so understanding about my struggles. After hearing that last note you played, Dean, she even offered me a place to stay with her."

"That's incredible!" Rose exclaimed, her heart swelling with joy for Tim.

"Wow, Tim. That's amazing news," Dean added, his eyes glistening with happiness for his friend. "We're so happy for you."

"Thank you," Tim replied, his voice thick with emotion. "I never thought I'd get another chance like this."

With that, he again walked away to join his friend on the dance floor. Watching them together, Dean and Rose couldn't help but feel moved by the profound impact their love had on those around them.

As the music continued to play, Rose turned to Dean with a question filled with curiosity and hope. "What happens after the last note?"

Dean smiled softly, locking eyes with her and radiating reassurance and love. "We move on to the next note, Rose," he said gently. "And we keep playing our song together."

Amidst the chatter and laughter of the lively wedding reception, Dean and Rose stood in a blissful bubble, their love radiating from them like a warm, comforting embrace.

The sweet scent of flowers filled the air, and soft music played in the background, adding to the magical atmosphere of the evening.

At that moment, they both knew their love had touched their hearts and those around them. They were two puzzle pieces that fit perfectly together, creating a beautiful picture of harmony and happiness. And as they looked into each other's eyes, they knew that no matter what challenges life might bring, they would face them hand in hand, one note at a time, making their journey together all the more special and meaningful.

Romans 8:28

We know that in all things, God works for the good of those who love him and have been called according to his purpose.

The End